Pumpkin Kisses & Harvest Wishes

THE THATCHER BROTHERS OF ACORN FIELD HEIGHTS

BOOK ONE

MAGGIE ELLIS

First published in the United States of America in October 2025.

Cover Design by InkVault Publishing

ISBN 978-1-953139-27-6 (Ebook)

ISBN 978-1-953139-36-8 (Paperback)

First Edition

10 9 8 7 6 5 4 3 2 1

Also by Maggie Ellis

STANDALONES

The Christmas Cabin Mix-Up

THE THATCHER BROTHERS OF ACORN FIELD HEIGHTS

Pumpkin Kisses & Harvest Wishes
Cinnamon Kisses & Forever Wishes
Secret Kisses & Twilight Wishes

Chapter One

AMBERLYN

I was drowning in irrigation hoses, and it was absolutely my own fault.

"Hold on," I gasped, trying to free my left arm from what appeared to be a garden hose mating ritual gone wrong. My blazer pocket had somehow hooked onto a metal coupling, my ankle was wrapped in at least two loops of green rubber, and I'd just knocked my elbow into the pump switch. Water exploded into my face with the pressure of a fire hose.

"Language, Amberlyn," Mom called from somewhere near the chicken coop. It was then, and only then, that I realized I'd been cursing like I was a fresh-faced 18-year-old freed from the confines of my parents rules. Only, I had passed that mile marker a long time ago and somehow missed the off ramp where my parents relented their control over my tongue and its choice of swears.

This was not how I'd envisioned my homecoming.

Four hours earlier, I'd crossed into Acorn Field Heights with my travel mug of overpriced coffee and my weekend bag packed with clothes that screamed, "I'm very important in Boston, believe it or not." The GPS had announced my arrival three seconds before I saw the town sign leaning at an angle. The population read 2,847, which was the same as it had been when I left eight years ago. Some things never change.

Other things changed so much you barely recognized them.

I'd slowed my rental car to a crawl when I hit Millstone Road, and that's when I saw it. The Avery Family Farm spread out on the left side of the road like a patient who had given up on treatment. Patches of bare earth showed through where there should have been orange abundance. The barn door hung crooked. The split-rail fence had gone gray with neglect. The porch swing on the old farmhouse moved in the wind —three creaks, pause, creak—exactly the way it had my entire childhood.

And then I'd made the mistake of looking right.

Thatcher Farms sat across the road as if it had been photoshopped into a different reality. Pristine rows of produce, a gleaming greenhouse complex that looked like it belonged in a botanical garden, and a modern ranch house. Everything was neat, organized, successful. Everything we weren't.

My hands had tightened on the steering wheel until my knuckles went white.

That's when I saw him.

Levi Thatcher walked out of the greenhouse carrying a flat of seedlings, his head bent in concentration. He'd grown into his height, filled out through the shoulders, but I would have known the way he moved anywhere. He'd always been graceful in a way that made me green with envy. Was that the right color? Anyway, he set the flat down, straightened, and wiped his forehead with the back of his arm. For one horrible second, I thought he was going to look up and see me sitting there like a creeper in a rental car, but he just turned and walked back toward the greenhouse.

Now, tangled in hoses with water spraying into my face, I wondered if maybe the universe was trying to tell me I'd made a mistake coming back.

"Need some help?" Dad's voice carried equal parts amusement and concern from the barn doorway.

"Nope." I spat out water and tried to twist free, which only made the coupling dig deeper into my pocket with a ripping sound. "I'm trying a new storage configuration."

Dad walked over and shut off the pump. The sudden silence felt

2

loud. He looked at me, and his mouth did that annoying thing where it tried very hard not to smile.

"Honey, they're hoses. They're fine the way they were."

"They're a liability." I gestured at the tangled mess with my one free hand. "This is a safety hazard, not to mention an efficiency nightmare. I figured it'd be better to organize by length and function, but apparently these have a personal vendetta against me."

"They certainly are cantankerous," Dad agreed, and started carefully unwinding me like I was a very large, very embarrassed cat. "You've got to know which end is which, or they'll get you every time. This one here, Lucille"—he held up the green hose—"has had a kink in it since 2019. She's temperamental."

"You named the hoses?"

"Just this one. She's a menace." He freed my ankle and moved on to the coupling embedded in my pocket. "There we go. Just let me... there."

With a loud tearing sound, my blazer pocket tore free. I looked down at myself—soaked, scraped, covered in mud, designer boots probably ruined, hair plastered to my face like a drowned rat.

My phone buzzed in my other pocket. Probably my boss wondering why I hadn't answered her last three emails. I pulled it out—screen cracked now, perfect—and thumbed it off without looking.

"When did you start naming farm equipment?" I asked because it was easier than asking any of the real questions banging around in my head.

"Around the time I realized I was having more conversations with hoses than people." Dad's voice stayed light, but something heavy fell across his face. He turned toward the barn. "Come on. Your mother went back inside to make some coffee. And we should probably talk."

The kitchen table was covered in papers. I'd changed into one of my younger sister's oversized hoodies and yoga pants—my weekend wardrobe was useless here—and wrapped my hands around a chipped mug that said "*World's Okayest Farmer*" in faded letters. Mom sat to my right, Dad across from me, and between us lay the evidence of everything that had gone wrong while I was gone.

"We're three months behind on the mortgage," Dad said. He didn't ease into it, didn't soften it. "Fourth payment's due next week. We don't have it."

I set down my coffee before my shaking hands could spill it. "How much?"

"Twelve thousand to get current." Mom's voice was quiet. "That's not counting the equipment loans or the credit cards."

"The credit cards?"

"Medical bills from when I threw out my back last spring." Dad tapped a stack of papers with one calloused finger. "Insurance didn't cover everything. We've been using cards to bridge gaps, but there aren't any gaps left to bridge. We're underwater."

I stared at the papers. *Final Notice. Past Due. Account Delinquent.* The words blurred together into a pattern I'd seen before in my corporate life, usually right before someone got fired or a business went under. But this wasn't some client's struggling restaurant chain or failing retail startup. This was home. These were my parents.

"What about the harvest? The Fall Festival's in three weeks. That's always been your biggest weekend."

"We don't have enough crop." Mom picked at the handle of her mug. "Bad harvest two years running. The irrigation system keeps failing—"

"Lucille," I muttered.

"—and we can't afford the repairs. Or the fertilizer. Or the seasonal help. We've been doing everything ourselves, but it's not enough." She looked at Dad, and they had one of those silent married-people conversations that happen entirely through eyebrow movements. "Eastbrook Development has been making offers."

"A development company?" I picked up one of the papers—official letterhead, corporate logo that screamed, *"We'll pave your grandma if the price is right."* "They want to buy the farm?"

"They want to buy the entire valley." Dad's voice went flat. "They've already purchased the Morrison place and the old Kemper farm. They're calling it 'Harvest Hills Estates.' With each property they acquire, they come back to the rest of us with higher offers."

"They're patient," Mom added. "They know we can't hold out

forever. The letter says they're prepared to offer forty percent above market value."

I did the math. Forty percent above market value for forty-seven acres would clear their debts, set them up for retirement, pay for Kenzie's college, and probably leave enough left over to buy a condo somewhere warm where nothing required irrigation or seasonal labor.

"So you're considering it," I said, not phrasing it as a question, but my parents nodded.

"We're considering everything." Dad spread his hands on the table, and I noticed how rough they looked, how the arthritis had bent his fingers. "This farm has been in your mother's family for four generations, but love doesn't pay mortgages. We've got Kenzie to think about. Her future, just like we considered yours. College isn't cheap, and she's got a real shot at a volleyball scholarship if—"

"You already know I don't want to go to college if it means selling the farm," Kenzie said from the doorway.

We all jumped. None of us had heard her come in. She stood there in her practice gear, gym bag over her shoulder, hair pulled back in that high ponytail that made her look about twelve instead of seventeen. Her eyes were red.

"Kenz—" Mom started.

"Don't sugarcoat it." Kenzie walked to the table and sat down next to me, her shoulder bumping mine. "I'm not a kid. You don't have to protect me from this. And I'm not going to college with farm money. That's not fair."

I tried not to flinch. I'd gone away to college on farm money. Maybe it was my fault they were drowning in red ink. Rubbing the back of my neck, I avoided my mom's gaze as she tried to get my attention, probably to reassure me that the thoughts I was thinking in that moment were not legitimate, even if they were.

"Kenzie, that's not—" Dad tried.

"This place is ours." Kenzie's voice cracked. "Amberlyn grew up here. I'm growing up here. You're going to sell it to some development company so they can build, what, a bunch of houses for people who want to live in the 'authentic countryside' but also have a Starbucks within five minutes? No." She'd hardly been sitting for thirty seconds before she jumped to her feet and stormed towards the door.

The screen door slammed—three bangs, pause, bang—and we all sat there in the sudden silence, listening to it settle.

"She's got your stubborn streak," Dad said to Mom.

"She's got yours," Mom countered.

I looked at the papers again. At the numbers. At the logo for East-brook Development. At the neat, typed sentences that made it all sound so reasonable and inevitable. Then I looked up at the kitchen I'd eaten breakfast in every morning for eighteen years before I'd gone away. At the spot where Mom measured our heights on the doorframe. At the window that looked out over fields that used to be full and were now emptying.

Across the road, I could see lights on at Thatcher Farms. The green-house glowed like a beacon. The barn was probably immaculate. The equipment probably all worked. When I'd left, Levi had stayed, and he'd built something that worked. Something that probably won awards and turned a profit and probably had working irrigation systems with properly organized, non-vindictive hoses.

I'd left, and look what happened.

"I can fix this," I whispered.

"Honey—" Mom started.

"No, listen." I pulled my phone out—cracked screen and all—and opened my notes app. My thumbs moved before my brain fully caught up. "This is literally what I do. I solve marketing problems for dying brands. A pumpkin patch is just a brand that needs repositioning and a solid go-to-market strategy."

"Amberlyn, this isn't—" Dad began.

"I've got three weeks of vacation time saved up. My boss has been threatening to force me to use it or lose it. I can stay through the Fall Festival. We'll create a marketing campaign, develop a social media presence, partner with food bloggers, and maybe reach out to some lifestyle influencers. We'll pivot from product to experience—farm-to-table events, agritourism initiatives, Instagram-worthy photo opportunities. Create a destination, not just a farm or pumpkin patch."

The words tumbled out in the language I knew best. My parents stared at me like I'd started speaking Mandarin.

"You want to Instagram our pumpkins?" Mom asked slowly.

"Instagram technically isn't a verb, but yes." I nodded. "I want to leverage your assets to create sustainable revenue streams that show viability to the bank." I was typing now, building a list. "We show them we've got a solid business model with growth potential. We catch up on payments. We save the farm. Three weeks is enough time to generate buzz if we execute properly."

"You have a job," Dad said. "A career. In Boston. You can't just—"

"I can work remotely for anything critical. My team can handle the day-to-day operations." Probably a lie, but I'd make it true through sheer force of will and very early mornings. "Besides, you're right. I need a vacation. When's the last time I took more than three days off?"

"2019," Dad offered. "When you had food poisoning."

"Exactly. I'm due. This is perfect." I looked at their faces—Mom's hope fighting with guilt and Dad's skepticism fighting with desperation. "Let me do this. Please."

Mom reached across the table and took my hand. Hers felt smaller than I remembered, more fragile. "You're sure?"

No. I wasn't sure. I had three major campaigns in crucial phases, a presentation to a client who could make or break my promotion, and a performance review scheduled for November. I had absolutely no idea how to market a failing pumpkin patch, and I hadn't set foot on this farm for more than a weekend visit in eight years.

But I looked at my mother's face and heard myself say, "I'm sure."

Dad cleared his throat. "We'd need to start immediately. The Fall Festival's October twenty-second and twenty-third. That's our proof point. If we can show the bank strong sales that weekend, maybe they'll work with us on a payment plan."

"So we have three weeks to make this place unmissable." I pulled the papers toward me, scanning them. "I'll need a full asset inventory, current customer data, any existing social media accounts—"

"There's a Facebook page," Mom said, already pulling out her phone. "Last post was June two years ago. It's Dad holding a zucchini."

"Really big zucchini," Dad defended.

"It's very impressive, Frank," Mom said in a fake formal voice. "Truly a remarkable specimen of Cucurbita pepo."

I bit back a laugh. "Okay. So we're starting from scratch with our digital presence. That's fine. That's actually good—a clean slate, no negative reviews to overcome. Tomorrow I'll go into town and reintroduce myself to local business owners, start building strategic partnerships. We'll need supplies. There's that hardware place on Main Street, right?"

"Hardware & Vine," Mom said. "Art Daniels runs it. He's been here since before we were born."

"Perfect. Local vendor relationships are usually the key to authenticity. Everything has to feel genuine, community-focused. We're not just selling pumpkins—we're selling the experience of supporting your local farming heritage." I was in my element now, building the campaign in my head. "We'll need a cohesive brand identity. Color scheme. Logo maybe. Definitely signage. Some kind of photo-worthy installation for social sharing. Oh, and we should see about getting listed on the fall foliage tourism websites. Do you have an email list?"

Two blank faces stared at me.

"We have a phone book?" Dad offered.

"Perfect. We'll start there." I made another note. "We'll need to build out the infrastructure, but I can set up automated systems. Email marketing, social media scheduling, maybe even a basic e-commerce component if we want to do online ordering for pickup. Streamline the whole customer journey from awareness to conversion."

"I don't know what any of those words mean," Mom said, "but you sound very professional and I'm very proud of you."

I grinned at my phone. "Looks like there's a TikTok trend about aesthetic fall activities. We could totally leverage that. Oh, and Instagram Reels. And maybe—" I paused when one of my sister's posts popped up on my feed. Another idea emerged from the others. "I'll find Kenzie and see if she'd be willing to help by being a social media coordinator." I turned my phone so my parents could see. Kenzie's video had fifteen thousand likes and over a thousand saves.

"That sounds like a good idea," Dad said, wrinkling his nose as he shrugged. "I certainly wouldn't do well in that position."

"You two just keep doing what you're doing for now while I get a list of tasks organized, and then we'll tackle it as a family. All four of us." I offered them both an enormous smile, the knot of guilt in my chest loosening. If I could help them save the farm, then maybe I could get rid of that little voice telling me it was my fault they were in this situation in the first place.

The kitchen clock ticked toward ten. Outside, rain started pattering against the windows. The sweet smell of overripe pumpkins drifted in through the screen door, mixing with the earthy scent of wet soil. Fall was coming on fast, and we were running out of time to save something that had taken four generations to build.

I looked down at my phone screen, at the growing list of tasks. My cracked screen made everything look fractured, which felt about right. I pulled my attention back to my parents, to the papers on the table, to the kitchen that needed saving. "Okay," I said, trying to sound like someone who knew what they were doing. "We'll make a proper plan. In the meantime, Dad, walk me through the full property tomorrow morning—I need to understand our actual assets and limitations. Mom, can you pull together the customer data you have? Even if it's just rough estimates of weekend traffic or approximate sales figures. And I'll have Kenzie start researching what's trending in the agritourism space. I need to know what worked for other farms."

They nodded, and something that might have been hope flickered across Dad's face.

"We can do this," I said, as much to convince myself as them.

Mom squeezed my hand again. "I'm glad you're home."

I was home. I was home, and everything was broken. I was home, and I had three weeks to prove I was someone who stayed instead of someone who ran. Three weeks to fix what I'd helped break by leaving.

Chapter Two

LEVI

The chickens wanted breakfast at six a.m., same as always, and didn't care that Amberlyn Avery was back in town.

"Morning, ladies," I said, scattering feed like I'd done every day for eight years. My phone buzzed in my pocket—third time since I'd walked out here fifteen minutes ago. I ignored it. "Agnes, you're looking broody again. We've discussed this. Yes, Gladys, your feathers are very impressive today."

My phone vibrated again. I pulled it out.

> Amberlyn is back. But I'm sure you already knew that call me - Love Aunt Caroline

> Hey Levi, it's Mayor Goldwin. Good news! I heard Amberlyn's home. Also, the festival meeting is on Monday. Should be interesting

And then one from my middle brother, Sawyer.

> your ex is back lol good luck bro

I shoved the phone back in my pocket and moved on to the goats.

Pepper head-butted my leg the second I opened the gate—her version of hello and also a complaint that I was approximately forty-five seconds late.

Gladys clucked at me, and Agnes pecked at my mud-covered boot.

"Yeah, I know." I measured out their feed. "And one of you ladies should tell Sawyer that she's not my ex. You can't be someone's ex when you were never actually together."

Gladys chewed the feed while giving me a look out of the side of her eye. It gave me the feeling that she knew I was splitting hairs.

Instead of facing the judgment of my band of moody chickens, I stepped out of their pen and checked the sky out of habit. The high clouds were moving in from the northwest, which meant that the cold front would hit sooner than the forecast suggested. Probably Tuesday afternoon instead of evening.

I pulled out my phone and logged it in my weather journal. When I'd finished, I scrolled up to last year's entry for the same date. Same weather pattern. Same migration timing. Everything was predictable and knowable if you paid attention to the details.

Unlike people, who left without warning and came back eight years later.

I finished with the rest of the animals and headed toward the greenhouse, but my feet stopped at the edge of my property line. Across Millstone Road, the Avery place looked worse in daylight than it had last night. Not that I'd been staring at it last night. Nope. That would indicate creepy stalker behavior. No respectable gentleman would climb a tree to see if he could catch a glimpse of someone he knew eight years ago. That'd be just weird.

Anyway, their barn door still hung crooked. I'd offered to fix it two years ago, but had been rejected. The fence had gone gray with neglect. And in the driveway, the silver rental car sat like proof that someone from the outside world had arrived to observe our little town's failures.

Morning mist rose from their pumpkin fields in pale ribbons, catching the light and turning everything soft for the ten minutes before reality burned it away. I used to love this time of morning. Used to meet Amberlyn at the property line when we were teenagers, both of us half-asleep and full of plans for how we'd change everything once we got to college. As I stood there, arms crossed, staring like a not-creep, a memory slipped through the fence in my mind.

Amberlyn, seventeen years old, sitting on the split-rail in cutoff shorts and an old 4-H t-shirt, bare feet swinging. Me, leaning against the fence post, trying to explain my theory about integrated pest management while she stole sips of my coffee, which was far too black for her taste back then. Did she still require an entire bottle of creamer to make it palatable now? Man, she'd loved the pumpkin creamer they brought in this time of year. The memory continued despite my squirrel brain diverging from the path.

"We could do this," she'd said, gesturing at both properties. "Combine the operations, implement all those sustainable practices we're learning about. Your technical knowledge, my people skills. We'd be unstoppable."

"Unstoppable," I'd agreed, and carved our initials into the oak tree to prove it.

That was before she'd switched her major from agricultural science to marketing. Before she'd stopped answering my calls. Before I'd realized that "we'd be unstoppable" actually meant "I'll be unstoppable somewhere else, without you."

My hands curled into fists in my jacket pockets, and I forced myself to turn away. The greenhouse needed attention. The irrigation system needed its morning check. Life went on, with or without Amberlyn.

I was calibrating the climate control in greenhouse two when Aunt Caroline appeared at the door, holding a thermos and a to-go container. She was small and wiry, with gray hair she kept in a bun and, to my dismay, she did that determined walk that meant she was on a mission.

"You're ignoring my texts," she said by way of pleasant greeting.

"I'm working."

"Liar. You're hiding." She set the container on my workbench and unscrewed the thermos cap. Coffee steam rose between us, smelling like the one thing she'd never learned to make properly—too strong, slightly burnt—but I'd never tell her that. "The whole town knows she's back. Dolores saw her at the grocery store yesterday. Ruth told her that Amelia Avery told her that Amberlyn is staying three weeks to 'save the farm with marketing.'"

"Good luck with that." I logged the climate data on my tablet and moved to the next zone.

"Levi." Aunt Caroline's voice went softer, which meant she was about to say something I didn't want to hear. If I weren't an adult, I would've plugged my ears and shouted "la la la" until she got the memo and left. My niece Maple could get away with that. It was a pity I couldn't.

"They're in real trouble. Eastbrook's been circling again. If they can't make the mortgage payment next week—"

"Not my problem."

"No, it's not." She poured coffee into the cap and held it out. I took it because refusing would just prolong the conversation. "But I know you. You're going to make it your problem anyway. It's what you do. You fix things."

"I offered to help. Frank said no."

"Frank has pride. So do you." She reached up and straightened my collar. She'd done it so often that I barely registered it anymore. "I raised you to be better than petty, but I also raised you to protect your heart. So, I will not tell you what to do. I'm just going to feed you and hope you make smart choices."

She left before I could argue, which was strategic. I ate the breakfast sandwich—bacon, egg, cheese on a perfectly toasted English muffin, nothing like the disgusting coffee—and tried to focus on the greenhouse calibration. But my gaze kept drifting to the window, to the view across Millstone Road.

An hour later, I was loading butternut squash into crates for the farmers' market when I saw her. Amberlyn walked down the Avery driveway, phone held up like she was recording video. She wore jeans and a cream-colored sweater, and—I squinted—heels. Actual heels that gave her another two inches. On a farm. In October.

I watched as she picked her way across the gravel, stepping around puddles. She made it to the road, looked both ways, then seemed to reconsider crossing. Instead, she turned and started walking along her side of Millstone Road, documenting every inch of her family's property with her phone. And then she turned her phone camera towards my property.

My jaw tightened. Actually, every muscle in me tightened. I should have gone back to work. Should have loaded the rest of the squash and ignored whatever nonsense she was planning. I mean, she'd ignored our entire town when she left, so it was only fair to return the favor.

But no. I tied my own noose. I picked up one of yesterday's prize pumpkins—a beauty at over forty pounds, a perfect specimen for the seed-saving program—and headed toward the road. I needed to photograph it anyway for my records. That's all this was. Documentation. Near the road. Where I happened to have a better angle for lighting.

The pumpkin was heavier than I'd estimated. I adjusted my grip, cradling it against my chest as I walked down the slight incline toward Millstone Road. Fifteen feet away. Ten feet.

Amberlyn looked up from her phone.

Our eyes met across the distance, and my breath stopped working. Close enough now that I could see her expression—surprise, then something that might have been nervousness, then that stubborn lift of her chin I remembered from a thousand teenage arguments.

Close enough to see that her eyes were the same dark brown they'd always been, that she still had those freckles across her nose she'd always hated, that eight years had carved tiny lines at the corners of her eyes but somehow made her more—

The pumpkin slipped.

I don't know if it was sweat on my palms or the angle or the way my brain just completely stopped working when I looked at her, but the pumpkin dropped from my arms. It hit the ground with a solid thud that sent it rolling directly toward the road. Directly toward Amberlyn.

"No—" I lunged after it, but the thing had momentum now, picking up speed down the incline.

Amberlyn's eyes went wide. "Oh—"

She stepped back, her heel caught on the gravel shoulder, and her phone went flying as she windmilled her arms for balance. The pumpkin rolled past her, crossed Millstone Road, and headed straight for the drainage ditch on her side.

We both ran.

My boots found purchase easily in the grass. Hers—those ridiculous heels—sank immediately into the soft ground near the ditch. She stumbled, caught herself, and we both dove for the pumpkin at the same time.

I got there first, my hands closing around it just before it could launch itself into three feet of muddy water. Amberlyn's hands landed on top of mine, and we both froze.

Her hands were soft. City-soft, no calluses, nails painted a neutral color that probably had some name like "Wealthy Beige" or "Corporate Mauve." Those were the same color, right? My hands were rough, dirt under the nails despite this morning's scrubbing, permanent stains from farm work that no amount of soap could reach.

We were both breathing hard. Her face was inches from mine, close enough that I could see her pupils dilate, could smell something floral and expensive that had no business being in a drainage ditch.

"Nice catch," she said, and her voice came out breathless.

I stayed frozen there like an idiot, holding a forty-pound pumpkin with her hands on top of mine, and tried to remember why I was supposed to be angry.

She pulled her hands back like she'd been burned, and the moment broke.

Right. She left me. Well, the town. But I lived there; ergo—

"Thanks," I managed, straightening. The pumpkin felt heavier now, or maybe that was just everything else.

Amberlyn looked down at her feet. Both heels had sunk into the soft earth near the ditch, mud coating the expensive leather up to her ankles. She tried to pull one free—it came out with a sucking sound that would have been funny if everything weren't so heavy. The second heel sank deeper when she shifted her weight.

"Need help?" The words came out more sarcastic than I meant them to.

"I've got it." She yanked harder, stumbled when it came free, and barely caught herself before falling. Her phone lay in the grass about ten feet away, screen down. She looked at it, looked at her muddy heels, and made a noise of pure frustration.

Then she just took them off. Pulled off both heels, held them in one hand, and walked barefoot through the grass to retrieve her phone.

"Heels," I said, keeping my voice neutral. "On a farm. Smart choice."

She straightened, phone in one hand, muddy shoes in the other, grass stains on her jeans. "I wasn't planning on doing fieldwork. I was just taking inventory of our property assets."

"Property assets." I hefted the pumpkin slightly. "That what we're calling pumpkins now?"

Her jaw tightened. "I'm doing competitive analysis. Evaluating market positioning and identifying potential differentiators."

The corporate buzzwords rattled around in my head, and my hands clenched around the pumpkin.

"Right. How's that working out for you?" I couldn't keep the edge out of my voice. "Found any good differentiators yet? Besides the crooked barn door and the irrigation system held together with hope and duct tape?"

"Lucille is fine, thanks." Color flooded her cheeks, and she continued before I could inquire as to who Lucille was. "We're implementing a comprehensive improvement strategy."

"A strategy. That's great. Strategies are important. You've always been good at those—strategic planning, strategic career moves, strategic exits when things got too complicated." Sarcasm dripped from my words.

Amberlyn flinched as if I'd slapped her.

"That's not—" she started, then stopped. Looked down at her bare feet in my grass. "That was a long time ago."

"Yeah. It was." I narrowed my eyes until she looked directly at me.

Her eyes did that thing where they went soft right before she got defensive. I knew that look. Had studied it, catalogued it, dreamed about it for more years than I wanted to admit.

"Levi—"

"It's fine," I cut her off, because I couldn't hear whatever explanation she was about to give. Couldn't hear her make it reasonable and logical and all the things that would make me understand why I wasn't worth staying for. "You're here to help your family. That's good. They need it. Maybe just keep to your side of Millstone, and don't overanalyze the work I've done over here."

"I wasn't—" She stopped, bit her lip. Tucked her hair behind her ear with the hand holding her phone, a gesture so familiar my chest physically hurt. "I'm just trying to understand what we're up against."

"What you're up against is eight years of neglect and a bank that doesn't care about your marketing strategies. I'm sorry, but you can't optimize your way out of this one. Farming isn't a campaign you can launch. It's work. Daily hard physical work."

She stood there barefoot in my grass with mud on her designer jeans and her phone cracked and her eyes shining in a way that made my stomach drop. For one horrible second, I thought she might cry. But then her chin came up, and that stubborn set to her jaw appeared—the one that had always meant she was about to prove me wrong about something.

"I know that," she said, voice tight. "I grew up here, remember? I know what farming is. I also know that good farming and good marketing aren't mutually exclusive. But thanks for the lecture. Really helpful."

She turned to go, picking her way carefully back toward the road in her bare feet. I watched her bend to avoid the steeper part of the bank, watched her pause to test her footing before each step. Too careful. Out-of-practice.

"Amberlyn."

She stopped, but didn't turn around. Her shoulders tensed.

I wanted to apologize. Wanted to ask her why she really came back, if she ever thought about that oak tree, if she remembered what we'd promised each other before everything went wrong. Wanted to know if seeing me made her chest feel like it was caving in, or if that was just my particular brand of pathetic.

Instead, I said, "Watch out for that exposed root. Two feet ahead of you."

She looked down, stepped over it without comment, and kept walking.

I stood there holding the pumpkin like an idiot, watching her head back up her driveway. She didn't look back. Just walked straight and steady until she disappeared around the side of the farmhouse, probably heading to the kitchen to wash her feet and add "inappropriate footwear" to her list of things to fix about her approach.

My phone buzzed. I shifted the pumpkin to one arm and pulled the device out one-handed. It was Sawyer.

> dude

I looked up and spotted him leaning against his truck about fifty yards down the road, feed bags in the bed. He'd clearly witnessed the entire mortifying encounter. He waved, then made a gesture that was probably supposed to be sympathetic but looked more like he was trying not to laugh.

> Go away

> cant. free entertainment. also you looked like you might cry. you good?

> fine

> thats what people say when they're not fine

> Get to work, jerk. Not paying you for the time you waste teasing me

I shoved my phone back in my pocket and turned toward my barn. The pumpkin was getting heavier by the second, or maybe my arms were just tired. Probably my arms. Definitely not anything to do with watching Amberlyn walk away again, this time with muddy feet and her shoes in her hand and that stubborn set to her shoulders that said she was going to save that farm whether it wanted saving or not.

Inside the barn, I set the pumpkin down. Then I sat there on an overturned bucket, staring at my phone screen, and tried to figure out what I was feeling. Anger? Hurt? Some combination of both mixed with the traitor part of my brain that was also relieved and excited she was back?

My thumb hovered over my weather journal, scrolled back without permission to October 1st eight years ago. The day she was supposed to come home for fall break during freshman year. The day I'd waited at the bus stop for three hours before finally getting her text.

> Sorry, staying in Boston this weekend. Big networking event. Rain check?

There had never been a rain check.

I closed the app and looked out the barn door toward the Avery place. Lights on in the kitchen. I could see movement through the window—her shadow crossing from sink to table, purposeful and quick. Probably already making lists, building spreadsheets, creating presentation decks about pumpkins.

She had three weeks. I gave her one before reality hit and she realized marketing couldn't fix everything. Two weeks before she got frustrated. Three weeks before she left again, this time with a clear conscience because at least she'd tried.

And I would be right here, the same as I'd always been. Same as I'd been for eight years. The one who stayed. The one who did the work. The one who built something that mattered out of duty and determination and the stubborn refusal to give up on a place just because it was hard.

Even if the person I'd wanted to build it with had decided I wasn't worth the work.

Chapter Three

AMBERLYN

I sat in the third pew—the Avery pew, same as it had been for four generations—wedged between Mom and Kenzie, trying to ignore the weight of approximately two hundred pairs of eyes drilling into the back of my head. The church smelled like furniture polish and old hymnals and the particular mustiness that came from buildings that had been standing since 1847. Pale October sunlight streamed through the tall windows, catching dust motes and making everything look softer than it actually was.

"Stop fidgeting," Mom whispered.

"I'm not fidgeting."

"Your thumb is hovering over your phone screen. Through your purse. I can hear you thinking about checking your email."

I pulled my hand away from my purse like it had burned me. Mom reached over and straightened the collar of my blazer—navy blue, paired with cream slacks, the most "responsible daughter returns home" outfit I could assemble—and gave me the smile that meant "behave or else."

"People are watching," she murmured.

"Why are people watching?"

"Because you're back."

Before I could point out that my return wasn't really ground-breaking news, the organ swelled and everyone stood. I grabbed the hymnal and made the mistake of glancing over my shoulder.

Levi sat four rows back and slightly to the left, wearing a dark orange tie that made him look like a responsible adult who definitely had his life together. Next to him sat a woman I didn't recognize—probably early thirties, wearing a crisp white blouse and a polite expression. She leaned over and whispered something to him. He nodded, whispered back.

Something uncomfortable twisted in my chest.

"Who's that?" I whispered to Mom.

Mom craned her neck subtly. "Oh, that's Dr. Li. Anne Li. Levi hired her as an agricultural consultant a few months ago. She's brilliant, apparently. PhD from Cornell."

Of course she did. Of course Levi had hired someone brilliant and professional while I was sitting here in my trying-too-hard blazer, nursing wounded pride and inappropriate feelings.

Reverend Borris stood up and welcomed everyone. "Beautiful morning. I see we have some familiar faces returning to us. Amberlyn, welcome home."

Every head in the church swiveled to look at me. I managed a weak wave. Mayor Goldwin, three rows ahead, turned all the way around and gave me a thumbs up.

"I understand you're here to help your family with their farm operations. What a blessing to see young people investing in our agricultural heritage."

From somewhere behind me, I heard what sounded like a skeptical cough. It might have been Levi. It might have been my imagination.

The service crawled by. When it finally ended, Mom intercepted me at the sanctuary door.

"Coffee hour," she said firmly.

"I showed face during the service—"

"Amberlyn." The mom-voice. The one that meant resistance was futile.

In the fellowship hall, the smell of burnt coffee mixed with the sound of seventy-five people trying to gossip quietly. The linoleum floor squeaked under my flats. Mayor Goldwin descended immediately.

"Amberlyn, dear." He was a solid man in his sixties with iron-gray hair. "We're having our Fall Festival planning meeting tomorrow night at town hall. Seven o'clock sharp. You should come."

"Oh, I don't think I'm really qualified to—"

"Levi will be there, of course." His eyes gleamed. "It would be good to have multiple farming perspectives. Creates healthy competition. We also desperately need help with our Instagram."

"I—yes, but—"

"Wonderful. See you tomorrow night, dear. Don't be late."

He walked away, leaving me standing there with the growing realization that I'd just been voluntold for something that would definitely involve seeing Levi.

I moved toward the coffee station, catching fragments of conversation:

"—three weeks, Dolores said—"

"—marketing, can you imagine—"

Then I heard the conversation that made everything stop.

Two men I didn't recognize stood near the window.

"Thatcher's been smart about it," the first said. "Buying up properties before anyone realized what was happening."

"How many does that make now?" the second asked.

"Five, maybe six. The Krestwick place, the Temker farm, that parcel off Route 7." The first lowered his voice. "He's consolidating the whole valley."

"Eastbrook must be annoyed."

"They're patient. But Levi's been one step ahead every time. Outbids them, closes fast." the first paused. "Though I heard he's leveraged to the gills. Taking out loans against his own property to buy everyone else's."

My hands tightened on my coffee cup.

"You think he'll go after the Avery place next?" the second asked.

"Has to, doesn't he? Can't leave a hole in the middle of his defensive perimeter. Besides, everyone knows they're struggling. He waits long enough, the bank will foreclose and he can buy it at auction."

"Are you okay?" Kenzie appeared at my elbow. "You look like you're going to murder someone."

"Murder at church is wrong, right?"

"Right." She drew out the word, scrunching her face as she frowned.

"Then I need air."

I pushed outside into the October sunlight, my mind racing. Levi was buying up farmland. And our farm was the hole in his empire. He was probably just waiting for us to fail so he could swoop in and buy everything at auction.

"Strategic planning again?"

I spun around. The man himself stood three feet away, still wearing that tie, hands in his pockets. Behind Levi, through the fellowship hall window, I could see Dr. Li talking to Reverend Borris.

"Just making notes," I said.

"Notes. Right." He glanced at my phone screen. "You know, most people put their phones away during coffee hour."

"Most people don't prey on failing farms, waiting to buy them up."

"What?" His eyebrows raised, and he looked at me like I'd spoken another language. "What are you talking about?"

"You're buying up all the lands. Competing with Eastbrook."

Levi scoffed, raising his attention to the sky as if it might give him an adequate response. When he looked back at me, a familiar smirk rested on his lips. "Well, you're good at that."

"At what?"

"Jumping to conclusions based on incomplete information." He took a step closer. "You've been here less than forty-eight hours. You really think you understand what's happening?"

"I understand that you've been buying surrounding farmland." I crossed my arms. "Creating a consolidated operation. And apparently our farm is the missing piece in your little Thatcher empire."

Something flickered across his face. "My what?"

"I heard two men talking just now. They said you've bought five or six properties. You're building a buffer zone. And we're right in the middle of it." The words came out faster. "You're probably just waiting for us to fail so you can buy our land at auction. That's why you were so hostile yesterday."

"Hostile? I saved you from a pumpkin."

"That you threw at me in the first place."

He pinched the bridge of his nose before staring at me like I'd grown a jack-o'-lantern as a second head. "You think I'm trying to force your family out."

"Aren't you?"

Levi gave a dramatic sigh. The kind adults give to children who have asked the same stupid question for the umpteenth time. "No, Amberlyn. I'm trying to keep Eastbrook Development from turning this entire valley into luxury condos and outlet malls." His voice stayed level, but something sharp edged underneath. "I've been spending every dollar I make—and plenty I don't have—buying up properties before the developers can get them. Whoever you heard is right. I'm leveraged to the gills. I've taken out loans against everything I own because if I don't buy these farms, Eastbrook will. And then they'll tear them down and pave them over and turn four generations of agricultural heritage into a shopping destination with a Cheesecake Factory."

"But I thought Eastbrook already had—"

"They got three before I started competing. I'm trying to keep them from getting the rest."

"I didn't—" I started.

"No, you didn't." He pulled his hands out of his pockets, then put them back in. "You've been gone eight years. You don't know what's been happening here. You don't know that Eastbrook's been circling like a vulture, buying up struggling farms. You don't know that I've been fighting them property by property, using every penny and every connection just to keep this valley from becoming another failed rural community that sold out to the highest bidder."

I opened my mouth. Nothing came out.

"For the record," he continued, voice getting quieter, "I'm not interested in your family's farm. I've got enough problems without adding your land to my debt load. I couldn't afford it even if I wanted to. I'm tapped out." He paused. "So you can go ahead and save it with your Instagram strategy or whatever you're planning. I hope you succeed. I really do."

He turned to go, and I found my voice.

"Levi, wait—"

He stopped, but didn't turn around.

"I'm sorry," I said. "I shouldn't have assumed—I just—"

"You just assumed I was the problem," he finished. "Yeah. I got that." He glanced back over his shoulder. "You know what the worst part is? I'm not even surprised. That's exactly what you did eight years ago. Assumed I'd be fine without you. Assumed staying here meant giving up. Assumed there were better things out there than what we had planned."

"That's not fair."

"No? Then tell me what happened. Tell me why you stopped calling. Why you left me waiting at that bus stop like an idiot every fall break, thinking maybe this time you'd actually come home."

"I—" The explanation caught in my throat.

We stood there in the church parking lot, three feet of asphalt between us that might as well have been three miles. Around us, people were filtering out, already talking about us.

"I should get back," Levi said finally. "I have a meeting about soil samples."

Wit Dr. Li. Of course.

"Right. Don't let me keep you from your very important meeting."

His jaw tightened. "You know what? You want to compete? Go ahead. Give it your best shot. But don't pretend you know anything about what I'm doing or why. And don't—" He stopped, shook his head. "Never mind. Good luck with your strategy, Amberlyn. I hope it works better than your conclusions do."

He walked away toward the fellowship hall where Dr. Li waited. I watched him go, my chest tight and my hands shaking.

Mayor Goldwin appeared at my elbow. "That looked intense."

"Perfect," I managed. "Just discussing the festival."

"Mm-hmm." He gave me a knowing look. "Tomorrow night should be interesting. Try not to kill each other before then."

An hour later, I sat at the kitchen table with a jar of peanut butter and a spoon, eating directly from the container while Mom made lunch.

"He could have just explained," I said around a mouthful of peanut butter. "Instead of being all mysterious about it. And I thought you said Eastbrook had bought up all those properties."

"I thought they had. I've been busy here. Haven't been into town much to hear the gossip."

"Well, thanks for that. Your misinformation made me look like an idiot." I took another bite.

Kenzie looked up from her phone. "But you made the choice to accuse him of being an evil land baron. Not Dad's fault it turned out he was being heroic instead. That's on you."

"I didn't say evil. I said monopolistic."

"Same energy."

Through the kitchen window, I could see Thatcher Farms across the road. Somewhere in there, Levi was probably doing something competent with Dr. Li while I sat here eating peanut butter like a stress-coping toddler.

"I need to check something," I said around a glob of peanut butter, standing up. Nobody stopped me as the screen door slammed dramatically behind me.

The massive oak tree sat on the property line between our farms, its branches spreading across both sides of the split-rail fence. The treehouse Dad had built when I was eight still clung to the larger branches —weathered but intact.

The treehouse where Levi and I had spent entire summers planning our futures.

Our initials were still carved into the trunk: A.A. + L.T., surrounded by a heart.

I climbed up, and from the treehouse platform, I could see everything. The Avery fields, the Thatcher Farms, and the entire valley spread out like a patchwork quilt, all of it threatened by development that turned places into products.

I understood why Levi was fighting.

Something crinkled under my foot. I looked down and saw a notebook poking out from between two floorboards. My heart stuttered. I pulled it out—spiral bound, water-damaged, decorated with drawings of vegetables.

I opened it. The first page was in my handwriting.

THATCHER-AVERY AGRICULTURAL COOPERATIVE: A REVOLUTIONARY APPROACH TO SUSTAINABLE FARMING

Below that was Levi's handwriting.

We're going to change everything.

I flipped to the last page. Our mission statement:

The Thatcher-Avery Cooperative will show that sustainable agriculture can be both environmentally responsible and economically viable. We will prove that staying isn't giving up. We'll build something that lasts. We will show that roots matter.

Below that, we'd both signed our names like a contract. A promise I'd broken without ever officially saying so.

My eyes got hot. I was still staring at it when I heard a voice from below.

"You know that branch you're leaning on is rotten, right?"

I looked down at Levi. Then at the branch supporting most of my weight. It was definitely rotten.

"It's fine," I called.

The branch cracked.

Okay, so maybe everything wasn't fine.

"Don't move," Levi called up.

"I just need to get closer to the trunk." I tried to shift my weight. The branch cracked louder. "This is fine."

"Amberlyn, just—"

I tried to grab the railing. My hand missed. The branch gave way.

I fell, except my foot caught in the fork of two branches and now I was hanging upside down. The notebook tumbled from my hands, pages fluttering. My jacket rode up over my head. Blood rushed to my skull.

"Are you kidding me right now?" Levi's voice came from below.

"This is intentional," I said into my jacket.

"Upside down. With your jacket over your face."

"Yes."

I heard him sigh. Footsteps crunched through fallen leaves.

"I'm going to help you."

"I can get down myself."

"You're hanging upside down from a tree." His voice was closer, almost directly below me.

"I'm fine."

"Amberlyn, just let me help."

My foot was losing circulation. My head felt like it was going to explode.

"Fine," I managed.

"On three. One, two—"

His solid hands closed around my waist, and suddenly I could breathe again even though breathing was actually harder.

"Okay," he said, voice very close. "Now twist your foot counter-clockwise and pull. I've got you."

I twisted. My foot came free, throbbing a bit. Then I was falling the remaining four feet except Levi was there, catching me, his arms tight around my waist as we both stumbled backward and hit the ground together, him breaking my fall.

For one second, I was lying on top of him, my hands on his chest, his arms still around me, both of us breathing hard. This close, I could see the exact green flecks in his hazel eyes, could count them if I wanted to.

"Thanks," I said.

"No problem." His mouth twitched. Almost a smile. "By the way, I came over here to tell you that you're trespassing."

"The tree's on the property line."

"You fell on my side. That's trespassing."

"Gravity made that decision without consulting me."

"Should have filed the proper permits with gravity first."

And just like that, we were eighteen again. Trading ridiculous arguments, finding the humor in everything, easy in a way that didn't exist anymore but apparently still remembered the muscle memory.

His hands were still on my waist. Mine were still on his chest. Neither of us moved. Oak leaves drifted down around us, catching in his hair.

"You dropped something," he said finally.

I looked over at the notebook lying in the grass, pages open to our mission statement. Our promises.

"I found it in the treehouse," I mumbled. "Our plans."

"Yeah." His eyes flicked to the notebook, then back to me. Something shifted in his expression. "We had a lot of plans."

"We did." Levi cleared his throat. "We should get up." He helped me sit up, his hands falling away. The October air felt cold where he'd been touching me. "Before someone drives by and next week's church gossip is about us rolling around in leaves together."

He stood and held out his hand. I took it, letting him pull me to my feet. He bent down and picked up the notebook, brushing dirt off before handing it to me.

"Here."

"Don't you want it?"

"I remember everything in it already." He stepped back, putting distance between us. Putting walls back up. "Your foot okay?"

I wiggled it. "Functional, a bit achy."

"As long as it's not broken."

"Do you see me screaming in pain?"

He chuckled at that. "Fair enough. Try to stay out of trees you're not qualified to climb."

"I'm qualified. I've climbed that tree a thousand times."

"Eight years ago. Things change." He glanced back toward his barn. "I've got to get back to work."

"Right. Don't let me keep you."

He started to leave, then stopped. Turned back. "For what it's worth? I'm glad you're trying to save your family's farm. And I do really mean that. This valley needs all the working farms it can get."

"Thank you," I managed. "I'm sorry. For assuming you were the villain, I mean."

He looked at me for a long moment, then nodded once and walked away, leaving me standing under the oak tree with our old notebook and oak leaves in my hair and the ghost of his hands still warm on my waist.

I looked down at the notebook. Opened it to our carefully drawn logo—intertwined vines we'd been certain would last forever.

I walked back across the property line, my head still spinning and my ankle throbbing. Through the kitchen window, I could see Kenzie at the laptop, Dad fixing the screen door, and Mom washing dishes.

Tomorrow night I'd go to the festival planning meeting. I'd be professional. I'd prove that marketing could save a farm, that I wasn't just playing at belonging here.

Even though every time I looked at Levi, I felt like I was eighteen again, full of plans and promises and the certainty that we could change everything together.

But what if nothing changed? What if I failed again?

I stopped on the porch and took one last look at the oak tree. At the treehouse where we'd planned to change the world. At the property line that divided what I'd left from what I'd found when I came back.

Kenzie opened the screen door. "You have leaves in your hair. Want to talk about it?"

"Nope."

"Cool. Mom made cookies for the festival meeting tomorrow. They're stress-baking cookies, which means they're extra good."

I followed her inside, brushing leaves out of my hair, trying not to think about the way Levi had caught me, the way his hands had felt, the way his almost-smile had made my entire body forget how to function.

Tomorrow I'd be professional. Tomorrow I'd have a plan.

But tonight I was just going to eat stress cookies and pretend that for one perfect second, lying in the leaves with his arms around me, I'd felt more at home than I had in eight years.

Chapter Four

LEVI

I had received texts from what felt like everyone in town. So when my youngest brother Asher decided to join in on the "pick on Levi" trend, I was ready to throw him to the hungry goats I was in the middle of feeding.

Have you SEEN the Avery Pumpkin Patch Instagram?? 2,000 followers since Friday. TWO THOUSAND. Thatcher Farm has 847 and you've had that account for two years.

quality over quantity

Sure, buddy, whatever you say

I shoved my phone in my pocket and tried to focus on the goats, but my brain refused to cooperate.

Amberlyn had gone all out. Professional photos. Clever captions about "authentic farm-to-table experiences." A partnership announcement with Harvest Moon Café. A TikTok video that had gotten ten thousand views.

I'd spent the same weekend fixing irrigation leaks and posting a detailed explanation of integrated pest management that got forty-three likes.

"This is fine," I told the goats, who were definitely more interested in the bucket I was holding. "Farming isn't about follower counts. It's about soil health and crop rotation and long-term sustainability."

The goats didn't care.

I pulled out my phone and opened Instagram.

Amberlyn's latest post was a carousel of photos: sunrise over their pumpkin field, close-ups of perfect specimens, a shot of their farmhouse that somehow made the peeling paint look charming instead of neglected. The caption read: *Four generations of Avery family farming. Come be part of our story.* 🎃 *#supportlocal #farmlife*

Three hundred likes already. It had been posted twenty minutes ago.

I checked my account. My last post about beneficial insects had forty-three likes. I'd posted it four days ago.

"You can't harvest what you don't plant," I muttered, which was something my father used to say and also completely irrelevant to social media algorithms.

My phone buzzed again from the other brother, or rather... menace, who shared my DNA.

> Aunt Caroline wants you at the café.
> something about "we need to talk" which is
> never good

Perfect.

Harvest Moon Café smelled like pumpkin spice and cinnamon—Aunt Caroline's fall menu in full autumn mode. The scent made tourists feel like they'd fallen into an autumn-themed fever dream.

Aunt Caroline stood behind the counter with her arms crossed. "Sit."

"I've got work—"

"Sit."

I sat at the corner booth. She brought over black coffee and pumpkin bread I hadn't asked for.

"Eat."

"I'm not—"

"Eat, Levi."

I ate. The pumpkin bread was excellent—it always was. The coffee was acid in a pumpkin-shaped mug.

"So," Aunt Caroline said, sitting across from me. "Amberlyn's back in town three days and she's already out-marketing you on every platform. How does that make you feel?"

"Fine."

"Try again."

"I don't care about Instagram followers. I care about actual farming."

"Mm-hmm." She took a sip of her own coffee, somehow managing to stomach the bitter, burnt taste. "Is that why you fixed their fence Sunday night? Because you don't care?"

I froze with another piece of pumpkin bread halfway to my mouth. I'd made sure no one saw me. I'd been so careful. "How did you—"

"Dolores saw your truck on Millstone Road at eleven p.m. You were out there for over an hour with your toolbox." Her expression softened slightly. "So don't tell me you don't care."

"Their fence was a safety hazard. The bottom rail had rotted through."

"And you just happened to have materials that matched their exact fence style? And you did it at night when nobody would see you?"

"I didn't want to make it weird. Frank said he doesn't want help, so I figured I'd fix it when he was asleep. What's he going to do? Speed up time and make it rot again? At least now it's fixed," I muttered.

"Well, you were seen." She pushed the plate with another slice of pumpkin bread closer. "Try harder next time."

"There won't be a next time. It was just the fence."

"You're a terrible liar, just like my brother was." She stood up. "Festival meeting tonight. Mayor Goldwin's planning something. Brace yourself."

It was my permission to leave, so I swiped the second piece of pumpkin bread and fled the scene. At least I could hide away in my greenhouse.

Or not.

By the afternoon, I was checking temperatures when I got a notification.

avery_pumpkin_patch posted a new video.

I told myself I wasn't going to watch it. I had climate controls to calibrate, soil samples to review, actual work that didn't involve obsessing over Amberlyn's content strategy.

I watched it.

The video showed her in their pumpkin field, golden hour light making everything look warm and perfect. She talked about choosing pumpkins, her voice easy and natural. The comments were already rolling in—people saying how charming she was, how they couldn't wait to visit, how authentic everything looked.

I closed the app and pulled up my own farm's account. Stared at it. Considered posting something—anything—that might compete with her aesthetic autumn magic.

Then I saw the hardware store's delivery truck pull up to the Avery place.

Posting could wait.

I walked to the property line and watched Art Daniels unload lumber and paint supplies. Watched Amberlyn come out to meet him, her laugh carrying across the distance. Watched her take a selfie with him, probably for another "support local businesses" post.

She was good at this. Really good. Making connections, building relationships, turning every interaction into content without making it feel forced or fake.

I pulled out my phone and texted Dr. Li.

> What's your professional opinion on social media marketing for agritourism operations?

> Highly effective when done authentically. Why? Need help with content strategy?

> Maybe. Let me think about it.

34

Alright, but just a reminder that I leave for Kansas in two days. Did you still want me to take a look at the Avery farm before I go?

Only if you can do it in secret. I don't want them to know I've been helping. If you do, let me know what their soil needs and I'll see if I can get my hands on it.

Ever the hero. I'll see what I can do.

I didn't respond.

That evening, the town hall basement was packed with twenty people crammed into a space designed for twelve. Flickering fluorescent lights, folding chairs that squeaked, and the smell of burnt coffee mixed with old carpet.

I took a seat near the back next to my middle brother, Sawyer, who had Maple on his lap. She was coloring something that might have been a cat or might have been a very elaborate potato.

"Uncle Levi!" She showed me a gap in her front teeth. "Look! The tooth fairy gave me five dollars."

"That's inflation for you," I said. "Smart investing."

"I'm saving for a pony named Sparkles." She said this very seriously.

"Solid goal," I told her.

Sawyer ruffled her hair. "We're still workshopping the definition of 'realistic expectations.'"

Across the room, Amberlyn sat next to her mother, taking notes on her phone. She wore dark jeans and a burgundy sweater, her hair pulled back in a ponytail. Professional. Put-together.

She looked up, saw me, and something flickered across her face before she looked away.

Mayor Goldwin called the meeting to order, which took ten minutes because nobody could agree on when to stop talking. He stood at the front with a clipboard.

"Welcome, everyone. Three weeks until the festival, which means we're behind schedule." He consulted his clipboard. "Booth assignments are finalized. Parking logistics are being discussed. And we have a special project that needs immediate attention."

He paused. Several people leaned forward.

"The corn maze," Mayor Goldwin announced. "Our biggest draw every year. This year we're making it spectacular." He looked directly at me, then at Amberlyn. "Levi Thatcher and Amberlyn Avery, you're co-chairing the corn maze committee."

The room went silent.

Then Dolores giggled. Actually giggled.

"I'm sorry, what?" Amberlyn said.

"The corn maze. You two have the agricultural expertise. You'll work together to design and implement it." Mayor Goldwin's smile was pure steel. "Unless you're saying you can't work together? Because that would be disappointing."

It was a trap. A beautifully constructed trap that made refusing look petty.

"Of course we can work together," Amberlyn said, voice tight. "Right, Levi?"

Great. Throw the bomb at me. "Right."

"Excellent." Mayor Goldwin made a note. He moved on to the next item, but I wasn't listening. Across the room, Amberlyn's jaw was tight, her hands gripping her phone.

Sawyer leaned over and whispered, "Starting a betting pool. Kiss or kill. What's your money on?"

"Your sense of humor needs work," I muttered.

Near the refreshment table, Quinn Fairchild—the new costume shop owner—was measuring the wall with a tape measure, probably planning a festival pop-up. Asher stood in the corner watching like a creep. I made sure to point it out to Sawyer so he could join me in teasing our younger brother relentlessly about his gawking.

After the meeting ended, people milled around drinking terrible coffee. Someone really needed to take the coffee maker away from Aunt Caroline. I was leaving when Amberlyn intercepted me near the door.

"So," she said. "Corn maze."

"Looks like it."

"We should probably meet. To plan."

"Probably."

We stood there under fluorescent lights that made everything look slightly green, both holding paper cups of coffee that had gone cold.

"Tomorrow?" she offered. "Afternoon? We could walk the field, figure out the layout."

"I've got Dr. Li at nine. Soil samples." I watched her jaw tighten at the mention of Dr. Li's name. Huh. Was she...was she jealous? "Afternoon works."

"Okay. Good. Happy to help the community."

"For the community," I agreed.

She looked as if she wanted to say something else. Her mouth opened, closed.

Mayor Goldwin chose that moment to announce leftover cookies, which caused a minor stampede.

When I looked back, Amberlyn was gone.

Chapter Five

AMBERLYN

"So," Levi said, standing at the entrance to the corn maze with his hand-drawn map and an expression that said he was already regretting Mayor Goldwin's forced collaboration. "Should we start with the main pathway or the secondary exits?"

"Main pathway makes sense from a flow perspective." I pulled out my phone and opened my notes app, where I'd sketched three different layout options complete with traffic pattern analysis. "I created some basic scenarios based on expected visitor volume—"

"Basic scenarios."

"—and I think if we adjust the entry angle here and add a secondary pathway that connects to—"

"Amberlyn."

I looked up. Levi had his hands in his jacket pockets. "Can we just look at the actual maze first? Before we optimize it?"

"I'm not optimizing it. I'm improving it."

"Right. Those are definitely different things." He turned and walked into the corn without waiting for me.

I followed, shoving my phone in my pocket and trying to remember that this was a professional collaboration for the good of the community, not a competition to see whose approach was more valid.

The corn rose eight feet on either side, rustling in the evening breeze. The air had that October sharpness to it, cold enough to make me wish I'd brought a heavier jacket. On the horizon, the sun sat low, casting long shadows between the stalks that made everything look like a gothic painting.

"The current design has three main pathways," Levi said, walking ahead without looking back. "This one leads to the center platform for the scarecrow display. The others branch off and loop back to secondary exits."

"What about challenge stations?"

He stopped walking. "Challenge stations."

"Interactive elements. Trivia questions, photo opportunities, maybe some harvest-themed activities." I pulled out my phone to show him my mock-ups. "Modern agritourism experiences require more than just—"

"It's a corn maze, not a theme park."

"It's a revenue opportunity that we're currently underutilizing."

"Revenue opportunity." He turned around slowly. "You've been back eleven days and you're already talking about my corn maze like it's a quarterly earnings report."

"I'm talking about it like someone who understands modern consumer expectations."

"And I'm talking about it like someone who's been running successful harvest festivals for eight years." His voice stayed level, but something sharp edged underneath. "But sure, tell me more about what my community needs."

"Your community?" I crossed my arms. "Last I checked, this was my community too. I grew up here. Same as you."

"And then you left. For eight years. So forgive me if I don't automatically defer to your expertise about what this town needs after a handful of days back."

I straightened my shoulders and pulled up my notes again. "Fine. Let's just look at your perfect design that definitely doesn't need any input from someone with actual marketing experience."

He started walking again. "Right. Because the most important thing about a corn maze is how it photographs for Instagram."

"You say that like it's not important, but social media reach directly correlates with visitor numbers, which directly correlates with revenue, which—"

"Which is all you care about. Numbers. Analytics. Optimization." He took a turn without consulting his map. "Some things matter beyond their market value."

"I know that."

"Do you?" He stopped and faced me in the narrow pathway. "Because from where I'm standing, it looks like you've spent eight years reducing everything to data points and profit margins. Including this town. Including your family's farm. Including—" He stopped himself.

"Including what?"

"Nothing. Forget it." He turned back to the path. "This section connects to the center platform. Follow me."

But I wasn't following anymore. "Including us? Is that what you were going to say? That I reduced our friendship to a data point?"

His shoulders tensed. "I didn't say that."

"You were thinking it."

"What I was thinking is that you made a choice eight years ago. You chose corporate success over everything else. And that's fine. That was your choice. But don't come back here and pretend you understand what matters to people who stayed."

"Stayed." The word came out sharper than I meant it. "You mean people who gave up?"

He spun around, and suddenly we were standing too close in the narrow pathway. "Gave up? You think I gave up?"

"I think you took the safe option. The predictable path. You stayed because it was easier than taking a risk."

"I stayed because my father had a heart attack two months before I was supposed to leave and someone needed to keep the farm running. I stayed because this place matters. Because community matters. Because some of us don't abandon people when things get complicated." His voice dropped quieter. "But you wouldn't know anything about that, would you?"

My throat tightened, and I couldn't get any words out.

"Nothing to say? Why don't you explain it to me? Explain why you stopped calling. Why you missed every fall break, every Christmas, every time you promised you'd come home. Explain why I spent too many years waiting before I finally figured out you weren't coming back."

"I—" The explanation stuck in my throat. Because what could I say? That I'd been scared? That the path I'd chosen had made success look so achievable while our shared dreams felt impossible? That I'd chosen the shiny path because I'd been terrified of failing at the hard one?

"You what?" He stepped closer, and I could smell soap and hay. "You were busy? You forgot? You found something better?"

"I found something easier," I said, and the admission hurt coming out. "I found a path where success was measurable and achievable and didn't require me to bet everything on a dream that might fail. Where I didn't have to worry about disappointing anyone or proving I wasn't good enough or—" I stopped.

"Or what?"

"Or watching you realize I wasn't as capable as you thought I was." The words escaped before I could stop them.

Levi stared at me. "What are you talking about?"

"You were so sure about everything. About our plans, about what we could build, about changing the world. And I just—I wasn't sure. About any of it. About whether I could actually do what we'd planned. So I chose something I knew I could do instead."

"That's—" He stopped. Took a breath. "That's the stupidest thing I've ever heard."

"Excuse me?"

"You were the smartest person I knew. You had ideas I'd never thought of. You made me believe we could actually do something that mattered." His hands curled into fists in his pockets. "And you thought you weren't capable enough? You thought—" He shook his head. "I spent eight years thinking you left because I wasn't enough. Because staying here, building something in this small town with me, wasn't impressive enough or exciting enough or whatever enough. And now you're telling me you left because you were scared?"

"I—yes. I was scared."

"Of failing?"

"Of failing you."

The corn rustled around us, the sound building as the wind picked up. The sun had dropped below the horizon now; the sky going purple with the first stars appearing overhead.

Levi opened his mouth. Closed it. Opened it again. "That's still stupid."

"You said that already."

"Because it bears repeating. You—" He pulled one hand from his pocket and dragged it through his hair. "Do you have any idea what it was like? Waiting for you? Hearing the excuses your parents made about why you couldn't visit? Checking my phone every day for calls that never came?"

I had to look away. "I'm sorry."

"Sorry." He laughed, but there was no humor in it. "Yeah. Okay."

He turned and started walking deeper into the maze. I followed because I didn't know what else to do, and also because the alternative was standing alone in the corn while the sun set and my emotional crisis spiraled.

"Where are we going?" I asked after two more turns.

"Center platform. So you can see the full layout before you decide how to optimize it."

"Levi—"

"Unless you'd rather just redesign it from your notes without actually seeing what you're working with? That seems more your style. Theorizing from a distance."

I stopped walking. "You know what? You're right. I left. I made that choice. But you made a choice too. You stayed in your comfortable bubble where everything's familiar and safe and you never have to risk anything because you've already decided that staying means being noble and leaving means being shallow."

He spun around. "Comfortable? You think my life has been comfortable? I gave up college. I gave up my own plans. I finished raising my brothers. I've been working seven days a week for eight years, taking out loans I'm still paying off, fighting off developers who want to turn this valley into luxury condos—"

"And you've been doing it all alone because you decided that's what staying meant. That being the martyr, the one who sacrifices everything, was somehow better than asking for help or admitting that maybe—

maybe—some people leave because they need to, not because they're abandoning you."

"That's not—" He stopped. "That's not what I think."

"Isn't it?" I stepped closer. "Because it sure sounds like you've spent eight years telling yourself a story where you're the victim and I'm the villain, and that's easier than actually examining whether maybe we both made choices we have to live with."

The wind picked up, sending the corn rustling louder. The temperature had dropped with the sunset, and I wrapped my arms around myself. Levi stood there in the growing dark, his expression harder to read by the second.

"You regret it?" he asked.

"Yes," I admitted. "At least, I have since I got back and have seen what's changed."

Above us, the harvest moon was rising—huge and orange, casting amber light down through the cornstalks. It caught in Levi's hair, turned his eyes more green than hazel, made everything feel suspended and fragile.

He stepped back, putting distance between us. "We should—we should head back. It's getting dark."

"Right. Yes. Good idea."

He turned and started walking. I followed like a stray dog.

Except after two turns, nothing looked familiar.

After three turns, I was certain we'd gone the wrong direction.

"This isn't right," Levi said, pulling out his phone. He frowned at the screen. "No signal."

I checked mine. Same. "How is there no signal?"

"Valley geography plus corn. Signal's patchy out here even in the best conditions." He turned around, studying the paths in the fading light. "Okay. We came from... that way? Or that way?"

"I thought we came from that way." I pointed in a completely different direction.

"That would mean we somehow circled back."

"Maybe we did."

"I designed this maze. I know these paths."

"In daylight. With a map. Not after dark."

He looked at me for a long moment, then nodded. "Fair point."

The wind picked up, colder now, making the corn stalks rattle and scrape against each other. The temperature had dropped at least fifteen degrees since sunset. I wrapped my arms tighter around myself and tried not to think about how we were stuck in a corn maze with no signal, no light, and no idea which direction led to the exit.

"Okay," Levi said, pulling out his phone again and turning on the flashlight. "We'll just pick a direction and follow it systematically. If we keep taking right turns, we should eventually spiral back toward the outside."

"That's actually smart."

"Don't sound so surprised."

We walked. The flashlight helped, but the paths all looked the same in the darkness—walls of corn on either side, dried stalks rustling in the wind, shadows that moved and shifted with every step. The harvest moon provided some ambient light, but not enough to see more than a few feet ahead even with the phone flashlight.

After the second dead end, Levi stopped and checked his phone. "Battery's at fifteen percent."

"Mine's at twelve." I pulled my phone out to confirm, and my stomach dropped. "We should probably conserve them."

"Yeah." He turned off his flashlight, plunging us into moonlight that suddenly seemed much dimmer. "Okay. New plan. We stop, we think, and we figure this out logically."

"I'm open to solutions."

"The center platform should be roughly in the middle of the maze. We were heading toward it when we got turned around. So if we can figure out which direction we came from—"

"We can't. Everything looks the same in the dark."

"Not helping."

"I'm being realistic."

"You're being—" He stopped. Took a breath. "Okay. We're not going to panic. We're stuck in a corn maze that I built on my own property. Eventually, someone will notice we haven't come back."

"When? Your farm is across the road from mine. Nobody's going to notice your truck is still here."

"Aunt Caroline will notice."

"How?"

"She notices everything. It's terrifying but occasionally useful."

Despite everything, I almost smiled. The wind picked up again, and I shivered hard enough that my teeth nearly chattered. Levi noticed.

"You're freezing."

"I'm fine."

"You're shaking." He started shrugging out of his jacket. "Here."

"I don't need your jacket."

"Amberlyn. It's forty degrees and dropping. You're wearing a sweater. Take the jacket."

"But then you'll be cold."

"I've got layers. You don't." He held it out. "Just take it."

I took it. The jacket was warm from his body heat and smelled like soap and hay. I pulled it on, and it was too big, the sleeves hanging past my hands, but it was immediately warmer.

"Thank you," I mumbled.

"Don't mention it." His moonlight silhouette seemed to stare at me for a moment, then away. "Come on. Let's keep moving before we freeze."

We walked, taking turns that led nowhere, doubling back, trying different paths that all looked identical in the darkness. The cold bit through even with Levi's jacket, and I could see my breath fogging in the moonlight.

"This is ridiculous," I muttered after another dead end. "We're two supposedly intelligent adults and we can't navigate your corn maze."

"In our defense, it's dark and we're both emotionally compromised."

"Emotionally compromised?"

"We just had a fight that dredged up eight years of unresolved issues. That counts as emotionally compromising."

"Fair point." I wrapped the jacket tighter around myself. "For what it's worth, I'm sorry. For what I said earlier. About you taking the safe option. That was unfair."

"Yeah. It was." He didn't say it meanly. Just factually. "But I get it.

You're stressed. Your family's farm is failing. You're trying to save it with three weeks and a marketing degree."

"When you put it that way, it sounds impossible."

"It is probably impossible." He glanced at me. "But I've seen your engagement rates. If anyone can pull off the impossible, it's you."

The compliment caught me off guard. "You've been checking my engagement rates?"

"I've been checking... um... yes." His mouth curved slightly. "It's impressive. Annoying, but impressive."

"Annoying?"

"You got two thousand followers in a week. It took me two years to get eight hundred."

I laughed despite myself; the sound echoing in the cold air. We turned another corner, and the pathway narrowed—corn growing close on both sides, forcing us to walk single file, then eventually so narrow we had to turn sideways.

"This definitely wasn't this tight in the daytime," Levi muttered.

"Maybe the corn grew."

"Corn doesn't grow that fast."

"Maybe it's aliens."

He made a sound that might have been a laugh. "The corn is conspiring against us."

"The corn is absolutely conspiring."

We emerged into a slightly wider area, and I realized I'd lost all sense of direction. The moon had climbed higher, turning from orange to white, providing more light but also making all the shadows look the same.

"Okay," Levi said. "I think we need to admit we're actually lost."

"I thought we were just temporarily disoriented."

"That was before. This is now. Now we're lost." He checked his phone again. "Battery's at eight percent. Yours?"

"Four. It drops faster in the cold."

"Great. Okay." He ran a hand through his hair. "We're going to be here a while, aren't we?"

"Looks like it."

We stood there in the cold, in the darkness, surrounded by corn that rustled its secrets. The wind picked up again, colder now, cutting through even Levi's jacket. I shivered, and before I could stop myself, I stepped closer to him—just for warmth, just for the practical reason that body heat was body heat and we were both freezing.

He didn't step away. Instead, his arm came around my shoulders, pulling me against his side.

"For warmth," he said.

"For warmth," I agreed.

We stood there like that, pressed together in the corn maze we couldn't escape, the harvest moon overhead, the frosty night air smelling like dried corn and earth and the particular sharpness of October.

"Levi?" I said after a moment.

"Yeah?"

"I really am sorry. For leaving. For not calling. For all of it."

His arm tightened around my shoulders. "I know."

"And for what it's worth—I never stopped thinking about you. About us. About what we could have built together."

"Amberlyn—"

"I just need you to know that. In case we're stuck out here all night and freeze to death and I never get another chance to say it."

"We're not going to freeze to death. It's not going to drop below forty."

"You don't know that."

"I absolutely know that. And besides, Aunt Caroline is probably already organizing a search party. She has a sixth sense for trouble.

"How would she even know we're missing?"

"I told you. She knows everything. It's her superpower."

I pressed closer to him, stealing his warmth, and tried to believe that rescue was coming. That we wouldn't be stuck out here all night. That this wasn't the universe's way of punishing me for eight years of avoiding him.

"For the record," Levi said quietly, his voice rumbling in his chest, "I never stopped thinking about you either, even when I gave up on the idea of you ever coming back."

My breath caught. "Really?"

"Really." His arm tightened around me. "Even when I was angry. Even when I told myself I was over it. I just—I couldn't stop."

I tilted my head up to look at him. In the moonlight, his face was all angles and shadows, his eyes dark and serious. We were standing so close I could feel his heartbeat, could count his breaths, could see the exact moment his gaze dropped to my mouth.

"Levi," I whispered.

"We should—" He stopped. Swallowed. "We should try to find the center platform. Get higher up so we can see better. Or maybe you could get on my shoulders."

"Right. Yes."

But neither of us moved. We stood there in the narrow pathway, pressed together for warmth, both of us breathing too hard for people who were just standing still.

The corn rustled around us. The moon climbed higher. And somewhere in the distance, I thought I heard voices calling our names.

But in that moment, I wasn't sure I wanted to be rescued at all.

Chapter Six

LEVI

I was not going to kiss her. I was *not* going to kiss her. But boy, I really wanted to kiss her. Until she opened her mouth.

"Do you regret it? Staying here? Building this life instead of the one we planned?" Amberlyn asked, staring up at me in the moonlight.

I thought about it. Really thought about it. About eight years hard work and stress. About building something that mattered but doing it alone after Sawyer and Asher left for college. About watching everyone I knew leave for bigger things while I stayed behind with livestock and irrigation schedules and a father who'd recovered but would never be the same until the day he died.

And sure, Asher came back after college, and Sawyer came back this year with Maple, but I was alone for a long time.

"No," I said. "I don't regret staying. This valley matters. These farms matter. What I've built here—" I stopped. "I regret losing you in the process."

Her breath hitched, fogging in the cold air between us.

I couldn't stand the awkward silence, so I did what I did best. I changed the subject. "Why don't you get on my shoulders and see if you can see anything."

"Oh. I don't know if that's a good idea."

49

I shrugged and crouched down. "Problem-solving mode. Gotta get out of this maze. Now, up you go."

She sighed, like I was inconveniencing her with the suggestion, but she grabbed my head for balance as she stepped into my palms. I lifted, and—*whoa*—for someone so tiny, she was all uncoordinated limbs and flailing elbows.

"Don't you dare drop me." She dug her fingers into my scalp.

"Never. But also, stop head locking me."

She wobbled like a drunk flamingo, one foot slipping off my shoulder. I tightened my grip on her ankle, but gravity had other plans. She yelped, and suddenly, I had an armful of Amberlyn as she tumbled backward, taking me down with her.

We landed in the dirt; her sprawled on top of me, cornstalks snapping like we were some kind of human wrecking ball.

"...You good?" I wheezed.

She lifted her head, spitting out a leaf. "That was a stupid idea. Only you would make 'climb me like a jungle gym' Plan A." She dusted herself off, cheeks pink. "Are you okay?"

I couldn't answer yet. My lungs were still trying to remember how breathing worked. The broken cornstalk lay across us.

"Levi?" She pushed up slightly, which pressed her hands harder into my chest. "Say something."

"Fine," I managed. "Dignity's bruised. Everything else works."

"We just broke your corn maze."

"Pretty sure the corn maze broke us first."

She was still on top of me, her weight warm against my chest, her hair falling around her face. My arms had automatically gone around her waist to break her fall, and now they stayed there because moving them would require making a conscious choice to let go, and I wasn't ready for that yet.

I opened my mouth for my next suggestion when I heard my name.

"Levi? Amberlyn?" Aunt Caroline's voice echoed through the maze, loud enough to wake every animal within a five-mile radius. "Where are you?"

Amberlyn scrambled off me like I'd suddenly developed the bubonic plague. I sat up slower, partly because I'd just had the wind knocked out of me and partly because I was trying to remember how to form coherent thoughts.

"We're here!" I yelled back, my voice rough.

"Very descriptive! Where is here?" Aunt Caroline responded.

Footsteps crunched through the corn. Multiple sets of them. Flashlight beams appeared between the stalks, bobbing as people approached.

Amberlyn stood up, brushing dried corn leaves off my jacket. Her cheeks were flushed—from cold or embarrassment or both, I couldn't tell. I got to my feet slower, my back protesting where I'd hit the ground.

Aunt Caroline emerged first, holding a flashlight that could probably illuminate a small stadium. She took in the scene—me on my feet, Amberlyn wearing my jacket, the broken corn stalk between us—and her expression went through several distinct phases: relief, concern, and knowing amusement.

"You've been gone for three hours," she said. "Three hours, Levi. Do you have any idea how worried—" She stopped, eyes narrowing as she swept the flashlight over the broken stalk, then back to us. "What exactly happened here?"

"We got lost," I said.

"You got lost in your own maze. What is the matter with—" She stopped. Pinched the bridge of her nose. Took a breath. "They're over here!"

"Where's here?" I teased her with her own words, earning a glare right before she shined the powerful flashlight in my face. I smirked at her.

Sawyer appeared next, grinning like someone had just told him Christmas was coming early. "Found them! They're alive!"

"How did you know we were missing?" I asked.

"Aunt Caroline called me saying you'd been gone too long and something felt wrong." He shone his flashlight at the broken cornstalk. "Then she called Asher to help navigate since he knows the maze layout. We've been searching for twenty minutes."

Asher emerged from a different pathway, looking annoyed at everything and this situation in particular. "Found the center platform. You weren't there. Checked the secondary exits. Weren't there either." He swept his flashlight over the destruction. "What happened to the corn?"

"We took some of it out when Amberlyn tried to climb on my shoulders."

"That was a dumb idea," Asher said.

"That's what I said," Amberlyn retorted.

Asher chuckled, glancing at her, his attention snagging on my jacket she was still wearing. He raised an eyebrow in my direction, but didn't ask. "Exit's this way. Follow me," he said, already turning.

We followed him through the maze, my teeth chattering now that the adrenaline was wearing off. Aunt Caroline and Sawyer brought up the rear, and I could hear them whispering—probably about me and Amberlyn and the broken corn stalk and whatever conclusions they'd jumped to about what we'd been doing out here.

They weren't entirely wrong.

Amberlyn walked next to me, close enough that our arms brushed with every step. She still wore my jacket, and I was definitely freezing now, but I couldn't bring myself to ask for it back. Not when she looked up at me and smiled that small, tentative smile that made my chest do things it shouldn't.

We emerged from the maze to find the parking area lit by truck headlights. My truck, her car, Sawyer's truck, and Asher's—all pulled in at angles like they'd arrived in a hurry.

"Next time you plan a corn maze consultation," Aunt Caroline said, pulling me aside while the others headed to their vehicles, "maybe do it during daylight hours with proper safety equipment."

"There's not going to be a next time."

"No?" She looked at me for a long moment. "She's still wearing your jacket, Levi."

"I noticed."

"And you're shivering so hard your teeth are chattering, but you haven't asked for it back."

"She needs it more than I do."

"Mm-hmm." Her expression softened. "Just be careful. I don't want to watch you go through that again. Losing her once nearly broke you."

"I'm not—we're just working together. That's all. It's the mayor's fault."

"Uh huh." She patted my arm, then headed for her car. "And fix that broken cornstalk before opening day. Safety hazard."

I watched her drive off, my body shaking hard enough now that I had to clench my jaw to keep my teeth from chattering. Sawyer walked over, still grinning.

"So," he said. "Amberlyn."

"Don't."

"I'm just saying, there are easier ways to spend time alone with a girl."

"We weren't—"

"You gave her your jacket." He clapped me on the shoulder hard enough that I nearly stumbled. "It's okay to admit you still have feelings. The whole town already knows."

"The whole town needs better hobbies."

"This is Acorn Field Heights. Other people's business is our hobby." He headed for his truck. "I've got to get back and make sure the menace is still asleep. Left her with Dolores. Text me when you get home so I know you didn't freeze between here and there. And maybe put on an actual coat before you get hypothermia."

He drove off, followed by Asher's truck, leaving me alone with Amberlyn. She stood by her car, making no move to take off my jacket even though we were about to separate.

"I should return this," she said.

"Keep it until you get home."

"Home is across the street and you're freezing."

"I'll survive. My truck has heat."

She walked over to me, and in the moonlight she looked exactly like the girl I'd fallen for under that oak tree. Same eyes, same freckles, same way she bit her lip.

"Thank you," she said. "For tonight. For telling me about your dad. For letting me climb your shoulders for rescue. For—for everything."

"Thank you for not breaking any of my ribs when you landed on top of me."

"It only seemed fair."

"Get home safe," I said before I could do something stupid. "Text me when you're there."

"I live across the road."

"Text me anyway."

"Okay." She smiled, then got in her car.

I watched her drive away, shivering hard enough now that my vision was starting to blur. My truck didn't have time to heat up as I followed Amberlyn's taillights until she crossed Millstone road and I went up to the house. From my truck, I watched her park in the long driveway, and a second later, my phone lit up in the cup holder.

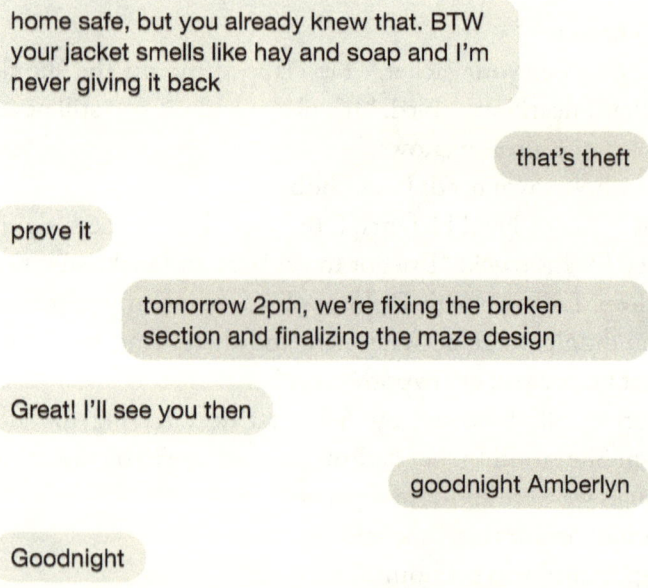

home safe, but you already knew that. BTW your jacket smells like hay and soap and I'm never giving it back

that's theft

prove it

tomorrow 2pm, we're fixing the broken section and finalizing the maze design

Great! I'll see you then

goodnight Amberlyn

Goodnight

Yep. I was in deep trouble because for the second time in my life, I was falling for the girl next door.

Chapter Seven

AMBERLYN

The town pumpkin carving contest was scheduled for Saturday afternoon, which gave me exactly thirty-six hours to figure out how to compete with Levi while wearing his jacket and pretending I hadn't spent Thursday night trapped in a corn maze with him.

"You're still wearing his jacket," Kenzie said Friday morning, watching me sketch pumpkin designs at the kitchen table.

"I'm giving it back. Eventually." I pulled it tighter around myself. Every time I caught the scent, I remembered standing pressed against his chest in the dark.

"You've said that three times."

"Because it's true."

My phone buzzed. I grabbed it too fast, grinning when I saw Levi's name pop up.

> weather dropped to 38 last night. frost
> warnings through sunday. bring actual warm
> clothes to the carving contest

> I'm from here. I know how to dress for
> October

you wore heels in the mud

I've learned. I'll just wear your jacket. It's pretty warm

Three dots appeared, disappeared, appeared again. Finally, he responded.

see you at 2

By noon, I'd settled on my concept: A pumpkin with a carving of a pumpkin holding a carved pumpkin of a carved pumpkin. Sort of like when you go into those high-end bathrooms with mirrors on either side of the sink, and your reflection goes on forever.

On the village green, long tables lined the gazebo, carved pumpkins already appearing as the contestants from the early round finished. Isla Mercado was setting up refreshments near a costume photo booth where Quinn Fairchild arranged props while arguing with someone on her phone. Mayor Goldwin assigned stations, placing me and Levi at opposite ends because we were "competitors."

I grabbed my carving tools and the largest pumpkin I could carry. It took longer than I expected to sketch the design, but I eventually got it to look decent.

At four, Mayor Goldwin rang an actual bell, and the contest began. I picked up my knife and made the first cut.

Across the green, Levi worked. Traditional approach. Classic jack-o'-lantern. It would probably be perfect because of course it would be. He'd be the first to remind me that he's been doing this for the last eight years. Well, over eight years, but still.

I carved for ninety minutes, pumpkin guts everywhere—seeds in my bra, stringy pulp under my nails, the sweet-earthy smell mixing with the sharp autumn air.

The third pumpkin within a pumpkin was where everything went wrong. The angle I'd planned didn't work with the pumpkin's natural curve. I adjusted, cutting deeper. The knife slipped. The cut went too far.

"That's interesting," a voice said behind me.

I turned. Levi stood there, his own pumpkin apparently finished, studying my disaster with a quirked brow.

"It's a pumpkin within a pumpkin within a pumpkin," I said defensively.

"It's definitely... something." He tilted his head. It currently looks like an explosion."

"I know." I set down my knife. "Your pumpkin's probably perfect."

"It's traditional. Nothing fancy." He looked back at my station. "Your idea is good. The execution just needs adjustment."

"You mean it needs not to be a disaster?"

"It's not as bad as you're making it out to be, and it's one of the more creative ideas here. If you can fix that tiny pumpkin, you'll definitely be in the running."

"You really think so?"

"Yeah. Don't sound so surprised." He started to leave, then turned back. "Your concept is more interesting than my traditional jack-o'-lantern. If you pull it off, it'll be impressive."

I went back to carving after watching him walk away, and the third pumpkin came together. When I stepped back at five-thirty, it actually worked. Not perfect, but good.

Near station five, I noticed Levi's little brother, Asher. His pumpkin had intricate vines and leaves carved in stunning detail. The man had serious artistic talent. He'd definitely be in the running.

At six, the judges examined each entry. They nodded at Levi's perfect craftsmanship, praised Asher's detail work, and paused at my pumpkin. "Interesting concept," one said. "I like it. Though the execution is uneven."

They deliberated, then Mayor Goldwin announced the winners. Third place: Asher. Second: someone's haunted house scene. First: Levi for traditional excellence.

"And special recognition for most innovative concept—Amberlyn Avery."

I accepted my certificate—not a ribbon, just a certificate—and tried to smile like this wasn't a participation trophy for trying too hard.

"Congratulations," Levi said as I passed his station.

"You're the one who actually won. You should be celebrating."

"Oh, I absolutely plan to rub this in Ash's face, the try-hard. And hey, don't downplay your win. You got recognition for taking risks. That's worth more than a ribbon." He held up his first place, and I didn't bother to stop the smile that crossed my mouth. "This is for doing something predictable well, which again, I'll brag about to my brother until he's blue in the face. But yours is for not being afraid to fail."

Before I could respond, Isla appeared. "Amberlyn, I've been thinking more about your offer to partner with my bakery. Let's do it. I think it's a great idea! What if we did a special pumpkin spice latte promotion? Cross-promotion on social media, tasting events—"

"Perfect! We could create a signature harvest package—"

"Uh oh," Levi said to Isla. "You've activated her marketing mode."

"Is that bad?" Isla asked.

"No. It's very her." He said it as a compliment. "I'm going to help pack up. Amberlyn, good work today."

Isla and I sat and talked about different promotion strategies for half an hour before she had to return to her bakery to save her assistant from the final evening rush. I was loading my pumpkin into the back seat of the rental car, which I had wisely covered with an old large blanket, when I heard voices from behind the hardware store. One was Levi's.

"—can't keep doing this without telling them," Art Daniels was saying. "Frank and Amelia should know you're the one paying for the feed."

My hands froze.

"They'd refuse it if they knew," Levi said. "Better Frank thinks it's a discount program."

"How are they doing with equipment repairs?"

"Tractor's fixed. I covered the parts, told them it was warranty," Levi said, grunting as if he were lifting something heavy. He probably was.

"What about the irrigation system?"

"From what I could tell, it needs work. Probably a few hundred in parts."

"Well, you're making me and everyone else look bad for how much you're taking care of them. Listen, order what you need to help them. I'll cover it."

There was a thud, and then Levi spoke again. "You sure? That's a lot of money."

My heart hammered against my ribs. I set down my pumpkin carefully, quietly.

"Levi, you can't keep doing this for every struggling farm. At least not alone," Art said. "You'll bankrupt yourself."

"I'm not trying to save everyone. But they're my neighbors, and the Averys have been here for four generations. My mom and Amelia were best friends growing up. They're good people who hit bad luck. I will not watch them lose everything because I have resources they don't."

"You have resources because you work yourself to death."

"That's my choice."

I stood there behind my car, hands shaking, trying to process what Levi had said.

I'd been such an idiot. He wasn't just trying to protect the valley from the developers at Eastbrook. He'd been helping my parents specifically. Making sure they didn't go completely under. Not competing. Helping.

He really was the hero, not the villain, and my parents likely didn't even know.

I loaded my pumpkin in a daze and drove home. Inside, Mom was making dinner.

"How was the contest?" she asked.

"Good. Levi won first place." I set my certificate on the counter. "Mom, Dad mentioned a feed discount—how long has that been running?"

"Since August, I think. I think someone said it was a loyalty program." She smiled. "It's been a lifesaver."

I went upstairs and pulled out my laptop, but I couldn't focus. I kept thinking about Levi in that parking lot, saying he wouldn't watch my family lose everything.

Levi texted me.

> Ash threw a hissy fit at third place. It was
> exactly what I had hoped for. lol

> I'm sure seeing a full-grown man act like
> your niece was the highlight of your day

He didn't respond right away, but when he did, I choked on nothing but air.

> Actually, the highlight of my day was
> seeing you

I stared at the message, thinking about feed payments and equipment repairs and eight years of him building something alone because he thought that's what staying meant.

> can I ask you something?

> Technically you just did. But you can ask
> something else. I'm in a good mood

> Ha. Ha. Why do you do it?

> do what? Pick on Ash? He's my youngest
> brother. It's my obligation as oldest

> Not that. Why do you help people. Protect
> the valley. fight for things that aren't yours?

The dots appeared and disappeared several times before a message finally came in.

> because someone has to.

> even when it costs you?

> especially then

I set my phone down and looked out at his farm across the road. At the barn lights and the life he'd built while secretly making sure everyone else's lives stayed built too.

I'd been wrong about him. Maybe I'd been wrong about everything, because the boy I'd left eight years ago had grown into exactly the kind of person I'd hoped we'd both become.

Chapter Eight

LEVI

Mayor Goldwin's idea of "unity" apparently involved forcing Amberlyn and me to co-guide a Sunday evening hayride with twenty townspeople watching our every interaction. I was starting to think the mayor took personal pleasure in watching the two of us squirm.

I stood next to the flatbed wagon at six on a Sunday evening, checking the weather—clear, dropping to forty-five by nine, wind from the south bringing bonfire smoke—and trying to focus on the trail I'd drive the tractor instead of the hyperawareness I had of Amberlyn. Unfortunately, the minute her headlights appeared, I knew it was her.

She parked and got out, wearing jeans, boots, and a heavy jacket that wasn't mine. Her hair was pulled back, and she carried two thermoses and a blanket.

"Coffee and blanket," she said, walking over. "Two-hour hayride in forty-degree weather requires supplies."

I took one thermos, fingers brushing hers. "You brought your own jacket this time."

"I wasn't ready to give yours back yet."

"So you're keeping it prisoner?"

"I'll return it once I have the ransom." Her mouth curved.

"How can I pay the ransom if I don't know what it is?"

She tapped a finger to her cheek, making a face to show that she was considering my question. "Hm," she hummed. "I suppose I'll have to actually come up with a ransom. I'll let you know."

"You're cruel."

She pointed to the jacket I was wearing. "Clearly, you have more than one. I think you'll live."

"So cruel."

People arrived. Families, couples, everyone looking at us. Sawyer showed up with Maple and the news that Isla was bringing cookies. Being the wonderful older brother I was, I then proceeded to pick on my middle brother about how he knew Isla was coming with cookies. Nothing gave me more pleasure than seeing the tips of his ears turn pink.

But sure enough, Isla arrived with a basket of pumpkin spice cookies, much to my niece's delight. Maple bounced around Isla, dragging her this way and that by the hand while my poor brother followed like a lovesick puppy. The poor guy. I understood how he felt.

Asher was nowhere to be found yet, and when I asked Sawyer about it (when he wasn't drooling over Isla), he mentioned something about Quinn.

So apparently, there was more older brother torturing for me to do when I eventually found my youngest brother.

When it was time to start the ride rotations, I helped Amberlyn onto the wagon and then climbed onto the tractor behind her. She'd be behind me to narrate the route the entire time. At least all I had to do was drive the tractor. She'd had to do research on the history of the town and the farms through which we'd drive on the hayride. I'd always hated homework.

"Ready?" I asked, glancing over my shoulder.

"For multiple hours with a ton of people watching us? Absolutely not."

"Same. But you have thousands of people watching you on social media. What's the difference?"

"Editing. Also, talking to a camera is easier than talking to people."

"Well, this first round is mostly people we know. Consider them your practice run. Looks like the next run is more tourist-heavy."

I started the tractor and pulled onto the road winding through our properties. The sun was setting, casting orange-gold light that made autumn leaves look like fire.

"Welcome to the Acorn Field Heights Harvest Hayride," Amberlyn said, standing carefully and holding the wagon side. "Tonight we'll tour local farms and learn about the agricultural heritage that makes this valley so special."

She was a natural at this, even though she was nervous. Her corporate skills translated well. She pointed out landmarks, shared founding family stories, and made the history interesting without being boring. The farms that were on the tour had decorated different sections for autumn, and orange and green lights twinkled around us.

The wagon hit a rut, and she sat down hard behind me.

"Sorry. Didn't see it," I called over the sound of the tractor.

"Uh huh." She leaned over the gap between the tractor and the wagon, poking me between the shoulder blades.

"Make sure you sit closer to the middle because if you fall off, I'm leaving you here until the next tour," I said over my shoulder.

She scooted toward the center and continued.

We passed her family's farm, and she shared stories about her great-great-grandmother, four generations of tradition, and her grandmother's recipes. By the time we got back, everyone was shivering except those who'd been smart enough to bring blankets. The line for the hayride wrapped around the side of my barn, and the locals who'd ridden the first round instantly jumped down and dispersed to their various booths and stations, giving some relief to those who'd stayed behind.

For three hours, Amberlyn and I drove the same route on the hayride, and I listened to her tell the same stories over and over again until I was pretty sure I could copy her word for word.

The last wagon group finally wandered off toward the bonfire, leaving Amberlyn and me alone on the empty flatbed. She slumped against the side rails, thermos cradled in both hands. Cold moonlight washed over her, making the tips of her lashes glow silver when she blinked.

I should've given her space. Instead, I slid across the rough wooden planks until our shoulders bumped.

"You're good at this," I said.

Her smile tipped sideways. "Funny. I felt like nobody was listening to me." She pressed the thermos into my hands before I could argue. "Here."

"That's not true. That one woman in the last group was asking all sorts of questions about the original house and the other old buildings at the edge of your parents' property."

"She was just being polite."

"Whatever you say. I enjoyed it. You did a lot of good research," I said, sipping from the thermos.

The coffee tasted like cinnamon and the cheap creamer she loved. I took another sip just to have an excuse to keep holding something she'd touched. Yup, I was pathetic

Across the field, Maple and a few other children shrieked with laughter, chasing fireflies, while the adults who belonged to them stood off to the side chatting. Sawyer and Isla, I noticed, were sharing a blanket awfully close. I made a note to tease him endlessly about it later. He'd certainly do the same to me about the woman next to me.

Amberlyn sighed, tilting her head back to watch the stars and forcing my attention back into orbit around her. "I forgot how quiet it gets out here," she murmured.

Our hands were inches apart. If I moved my pinky slightly, we'd be touching. I didn't. Neither did she. But I was aware of that space in a way that felt like everything.

"Can I ask you something?" Amberlyn said after a moment.

"Again, you just did, but I don't know how much longer I can let that slide. You're using up your allotted questions. But I guess I'll give you a pass for tonight since you did such a great job."

"You are impossible." She chuckled, nudging me with her shoulder.

"That wasn't a question."

"Fine, here's my question. What was it like? Taking over the farm at eighteen. Giving up college and everything you'd planned."

"Terrifying," I said without hesitation. "I didn't know what I was doing. Dad tried to help from the hospital, but there's only so much you can explain over the phone. Aunt Caroline was dealing with her own grief after Mom died. So I just figured it out. Made mistakes. Fixed them. Made more mistakes."

"You were eighteen."

"Yeah. Felt about twelve most days." I watched the road ahead. "The worst part wasn't the work. It was watching everyone else leave. You, then Sawyer, then Asher, then everyone headed to college or cities. And I was here, learning crop rotations and equipment maintenance and how to keep animals alive through winter."

"Were you lonely?"

"I had Aunt Caroline and folks in town. But yeah," I said finally. "Still am, sometimes. Even with my brothers back. They've changed, and so have I. And I think there's a difference between having people nearby and having someone who understands you."

She was quiet. Then she shifted, and her hand moved closer to mine. Not touching. Just closer.

"For what it's worth," she said, "I think you built something incredible."

"You said I took the easy path."

"I was wrong. I was defending my choices by making yours look small." She looked at the stars instead of me. "What you did was harder than anything I've done. You stayed when everyone else left. You built something that mattered. You protected this valley. You protected my parents."

"I saw you lurking after the carving contest. I didn't realize you were there until I'd already admitted to the feed payments. I know you know, but I'd appreciate it if you didn't tell your parents."

"I won't. I agree that they don't want handouts, even if that's what they need right now." She finally looked at me. "Thank you for looking after them when I left." Amberlyn paused and bit her lip. "Can I tell you something?" she said after a moment.

"Okay."

"I hate my job." The confession came out quiet. "I'm good at it. Make decent money, have a promotion track, everyone thinks I'm successful. But I wake up every morning dreading it. Creating campaigns for products I don't care about, measuring success by metrics that mean nothing real. I've been ignoring my boss's emails and calls since I got here, blaming it on poor reception and internet."

"Then why do you do it?"

"Because I'm good at it. Because it's safe. Because eight years ago I chose this path, and I've been too scared to admit I chose wrong." She pulled her jacket tighter. "When I came back, it was supposed to be temporary. Three weeks, then back to Boston and my real life. But the longer I'm here, the more I realize—that's not my real life. This is. Or it was. Or it could be again."

My chest tightened. "Could be?"

"I have one more week here. Then I'm supposed to go back to my apartment and my job and my life where I know exactly what I'm doing even if I hate it." She looked at me, eyes shining in the darkness. "But when I think about leaving—it feels wrong. Like making the same mistake twice."

"So don't leave."

"It's not that simple. I have a career, a lease, a life there—"

"You know you could have those here too, if that's what you wanted."

She was quiet. "I know." Her pinky finger moved that last inch and touched mine.

I thought about eight years of watching her parents struggle. About four generations ending because of bad luck. About the girl I'd loved who'd left and come back changed but somehow still the same. Interlocking my pinky with hers, I watched her watch the stars, and made a small secret wish that she might choose to stay this time.

Chapter Nine

AMBERLYN

The longer I stayed in Acorn Field Heights, the more I remembered how much the little town obsessed over fall. There was the pumpkin carving competition, hayride night, and tonight was the annual harvest moon dance. Not to mention the enormous festival in a week. It was a wonder anyone got anything done in the month of October.

I arrived at the dance at seven, wearing a maroon dress with boots and a cardigan. The village green gazebo glowed with string lights, decorated with cornstalks and pumpkins. A band—fiddle, guitar, bass—warmed up while people gathered around refreshment tables where Levi's Aunt Caroline ladled cider that smelled suspiciously strong.

I was heading straight for the cider when I heard my name called.

"You came," a voice said behind me.

I turned. Levi stood there in dark jeans and a button-down, hands in his pockets, looking at me like he'd been waiting.

"I said I would."

"You look nice."

"Thanks. You too." I gestured at the gazebo. "Did you help with this?"

"Nope. I volunteered Ash for it. I think he's planning to give me cow patties for Christmas as a big stinky thank you."

"And you know what, I think he actually would."

Levi flashed a brilliant smile at me. "He definitely would. But he'll also thank me, because I'm pretty sure Quinn was supposed to help with this too."

"Isn't she new? I thought being voluntold to do fall-related things was purely for the poor locals like us." I gestured to him and me.

"Mayor Goldwin has no mercy, it seems." He held out his hand. "Now, it is called the harvest moon dance, so would like to dance with me?"

I took his hand, and he led me onto the gazebo floor where couples were already two-stepping. His hand settled on my waist, mine on his shoulder, and we were suddenly close enough that I could smell soap and autumn air.

"Two-step is easy," he said. "Quick-quick-slow-slow. Follow my lead."

I tried. Stepped on his foot immediately.

"Sorry."

"They're steel-toed. Stomp away. And don't think so hard. Just feel the rhythm and have fun."

I stopped trying to think and started responding to his hand on my waist, the way he guided me through turns. After a minute, I realized we were actually dancing.

"See?" he said. "You're doing it."

"I'm trying not to think about everyone watching."

"Everyone. The entire town."

"Not helping."

"Sorry." That small almost-smile.

The music was fast and bright, but Levi moved with an easy confidence I was definitely not at all jealous of. He spun me under his arm—I thankfully didn't trip—then pulled me back in closer than before. The fiddles sawed faster, and Levi grinned when I yelped as we picked up speed.

"I can't keep up!"

"Yes, you can," he countered, steering us through the growing crowd of dancers like he knew exactly where every step would land. My breath came quick from laughing, my boots scuffing against the wooden floor. People blurred around us—Mayor Goldwin clapping in time, Aunt Caroline raising a sloshing cup in our direction, my parents also spinning around the dance floor nearby—but I barely noticed.

The song ended with a final spirited note, and we stood there a beat too long, both still humming with the rhythm. His thumb brushed my waist.

Neither of us moved. My hand still rested on his shoulder, his on my waist. My boots scuffed against the wooden floor as I shifted, and Levi's grip tightened just enough to steady me.

I looked up at him. Levi had always been tall, but the gangly boy from my memories had filled out. His shoulders were broad now, his arms solid from years of hard work on the farm. His jaw was sharper, shadowed with stubble that made him look older, more rugged. And his eyes—those same dark eyes that used to follow me across the yard when we were kids—still held that same intensity, but now they seemed deeper, like they'd seen more than they ever should have.

"What?" he asked, his voice low.

"Nothing." I shook my head, my cheeks warming. "Just... you grew up."

"You're just noticing that now?" He raised an eyebrow, that almost-smile tugging at his lips. "If you didn't notice, so did you."

"I don't have tree trunks for arms, thanks," I muttered, and he laughed, the sound rumbling through his chest. I could feel it where my hand rested.

Mayor Goldwin rang a bell. "Time for the traditional Harvest Moon Partner Dance! Remember—promises made under the harvest moon are binding!"

Levi squeezed my waist, and not for the first time, I was grateful not to be ticklish. "One more dance?" Levi asked.

I nodded, and we moved closer as the band started something slower. Close enough that I could feel his heartbeat, see the exact way he was looking at me.

"Levi, you know I'm only here for one more week."

"I know."

"After that, I'm supposed to go back to Boston. To the job I hate and my apartment and my life."

"I know that too."

"But... but I don't want to." The words escaped before I could stop them. "I don't want to go back. I don't want to leave you again. I don't want to spend another eight years wondering what would have happened if I'd been brave enough to stay."

His hand tightened on my waist. "So stay."

"It's not that simple."

"Why not?"

"Because I have a lease and a career and responsibilities—"

"And you hate your job. Why go back to something making you unhappy when you could stay here and build something that matters?"

"Because staying is scary. What if I try, but fail? What if I give up everything in Boston and discover I can't make it work here? What if—" I stopped, and my voice came out small. "What if you realize I'm not the person you've been hoping would come back?"

He stopped dancing. We stood there while couples moved around us, and he looked at me like I'd said the stupidest thing he'd ever heard.

"Amberlyn, every single day, you've been exactly the person I've been hoping would come back."

"Really?"

"Really." His hand came up to my face, tucking hair behind my ear. "You're exactly the person I'd hoped would come back, because you're you."

"But I broke your heart."

"Yeah. And I'd let you do it again if it meant having you here now."

The harvest moon glowed above us. The fiddle played something sweet.

"I never stopped thinking about you," I said. "Every time I saw farmland, every autumn, every pumpkin—I thought about you and what we'd planned and what I'd given up."

"So don't give it up again. Stay. Please. I know it's scary, and you'd be giving up a lot. But stay anyway. Stay and help me save this valley. Stay and build what we planned when we were eighteen. Stay because —" He stopped.

"Because what?"

"Because I'm in love with you. Still. Again. I don't know if I ever stopped. I know I never told you, but—"

"Levi," I whispered. "I'm in love with you too."

He smiled—actually smiled, transforming his entire face—and kissed me.

His hands cupped my face. His lips were soft and warm and tasted like cider. The kiss was sweet and careful and felt like coming home after eight years lost.

When we pulled apart, the entire gazebo was watching. Sawyer and Asher grinned. Aunt Caroline wiped her eyes. My parents were beaming..

"Everyone's staring," I said against his mouth.

"It's a nosy town."

He kissed me again, and I kissed him back, and people cheered, and for the first time in eight years I wasn't thinking about what I should do or what made sense. I was just here, now, with him, choosing something that felt right instead of safe.

When we finally stopped—mostly because of the whistling—Levi rested his forehead against mine.

"So?" he said. "Are you staying?"

"I have to go back to Boston first. I'll leave right away. I'll give notice, break my lease, pack up my life. But I can't just abandon everything without closing that chapter."

"I know."

"But then—" I took a breath. Made the choice I should have made eight years ago. "But then I'm coming back. For real. Not three weeks. For good."

His arms tightened. "Yeah?"

"Yeah. I'm sure."

"When will you leave?"

"Wednesday morning if I can get a flight. I'll put in my two weeks' notice and aim to be back the first week of November."

"Two weeks." His expression shifted—something like pain crossing his face before he hid it. "That's a long time."

"Eight years was a long time. Two weeks is nothing. Besides, I'll come back for the festival weekend. Saturday and Sunday."

"Five days, then." He kissed me softly. "You're really coming back?"

"I promise. Under the harvest moon, which Mayor Goldwin says is binding."

"Legally binding in this town."

"Is it actually?"

"Should be."

We stayed for another hour, dancing while I stepped on his feet many more times. When people started leaving, Levi walked me to my car, his hand in mine.

"Wednesday," he said. "That's two days."

"I know."

"And then two weeks."

"But I'll be back for the festival."

He looked at me, and something in his expression made my chest ache. "Just—come back. Please."

"I will. I promise."

He kissed me again, as if he couldn't get enough of me. Like he was trying to memorize the feel of me. The taste of me. I couldn't blame him. I wanted to do the same. He eventually opened my car door and watched me drive away.

Chapter Ten

LEVI

Things were perfect for exactly thirty-six hours. Monday night after the dance, I'd driven home with the taste of her kiss still on my lips and the promise that she was coming back. Tuesday morning, I'd checked the weather—clear, dropping to thirty-eight overnight, first frost warning for Wednesday—and told myself two weeks was nothing. I'd waited eight years. I could wait a few more days.

Then Tuesday afternoon, the headhunter called her.

I tossed the last handful of hay into the goat pen just as Amberlyn's phone rang. She'd been trailing behind me all morning, her tennis shoes kicking up dust. The goats mobbed her, butting their heads against her legs like she was holding out on them.

"I promise, I don't have food," she laughed, scratching the knobs between one of their horns. Her phone rang again, and her whole body went rigid. "Oh, I should take this."

"Of course." I pretended not to notice the way her voice dropped when she answered, the way she turned her back on me like I wouldn't be able to hear her from ten feet away.

"Yes, I'm still in Boston as far as HR is concerned..." A pause. "Really? That's very kind, but... How much?" Another pause, and her fingers tightened around the fence post. "That's a lot."

Pepper, one of the more stubborn goats, shoved her nose into Amberlyn's pocket. Normally, she'd laugh and shove her away. Now, she didn't even seem to notice.

"Listen, let me look at the details, and I'll speak with you when I get back in the office on Thursday. Yes. Of course. Thanks, you too. Bye bye."

She hung up and didn't even look at me, her thumbs flying over her screen. I tossed another handful of hay harder than necessary, and one of the younger goats startled.

"What's happening on Thursday?" I kept my voice light, but she flinched as if I'd yelled.

"I've got a meeting." She tucked her phone away and forced a smile. "So, how many goats did you say we're taking to the festival?"

"Don't change the subject. What's the meeting for?" My stomach twisted into knots before she even answered.

She sighed, shoving her phone into her back pocket. "It's a job promotion, Levi. A good one. Way better than what I'm doing now."

"But you're planning to put your two weeks in."

She rubbed her temples. "Look, I told you I'm going back to Boston to wrap things up. That hasn't changed."

"But it might on Thursday, right? Wrap things up with the job you're in now so you can take a promotion."

Her jaw tightened. "I just said I'll look at the details. That's not—"

"Am I just supposed to sit here and wait for you to decide if coming back is convenient?" The words tasted vile the second they left my mouth, but I couldn't stop them. "Again."

Her expression shattered. "I said I'm coming back."

"You said that eight years ago too, remember? And I told you I waited. Every year. Is that what this is going to be again? Me waiting like an obedient dog?"

"You have to trust me."

"Well, I don't."

Hurt flashed across her face, and I opened my mouth—to say what, I wasn't even sure—when my phone buzzed violently in my pocket.

Sawyer's name flashed across the screen.

"Answer it," she hissed, her voice brittle. "I'm leaving." She turned on her heel and walked toward her parent's house, shoulders rigid.

I hit accept.

Before I could even speak, Sawyer's voice cut through, ragged and raw. "She's filing for full custody."

"What? Who?" I realized how dumb the question was as soon as I asked it. I knew who.

"Jen's lawyer just called." Sawyer's breath hitched. "Said unless I can prove I have 'stable employment,' they're taking Maple. Said working for you part-time isn't gonna cut it."

My chest caved.

"Levi, I can't—I can't lose her." His voice cracked. "I have to find something else."

"Yeah," I managed, even though I could already feel the familiar sense of panic creeping through my veins. "Yeah, of course. I totally understand. You've got to do what's right for Maple. I'll... I'll find someone to take your place. There's got to be a kid down at the high school looking for part-time hours."

"I'm so sorry, man. Really. I know things are tight, but I—I just..." His voice broke, and I recognized the sound of my brother crying.

"Hey, it's gonna be okay, Sawyer. Take care of your family. I'll take care of myself." Like I always did. Alone. "Maybe talk to the mayor, see if they have any positions open in town hall. That'll look good, right? Sawyer?" I called his name again when the only thing I could hear was him struggling to breathe. I was about to ask where he was so I could go comfort him in person when a small voice piped up in the background.

"Why are you crying, Daddy?"

Sawyer muffled the phone, but I still heard his shaky "It's okay, pumpkin" before he came back on. "Levi, I'll call you tonight."

"Yeah, man. Whatever you need."

The line went dead.

I turned. Amberlyn was gone. Just the goats, staring at me like I'd betrayed them by not producing more food.

Wednesday morning came with the first frost of the season. I woke at five to ice crystallizing on the windows in delicate patterns, my breath visible in the cold bedroom air. The radio announced frost warnings and temperatures dropping to thirty-two degrees, advising farmers to protect sensitive plants. I checked the greenhouse. Everything was fine; the heaters had kicked on automatically.

At eight, I saw her load her two suitcases, her mom helping, and I stood at my window watching like the pathetic person I'd apparently become.

I wasn't ready for her to leave, but I was also afraid my pride wouldn't let me say that. Not knowing that she might not stay again.

So I stayed where I was and didn't go say goodbye like my legs wanted me to.

I lingered by the window, my fingers tapping against the cold glass. Her mom, dad, and sister waved from the porch, and I could just make out the tension in Amberlyn's shoulders as she climbed into the driver's seat. She didn't look back at the house, didn't glance toward the farm or, more importantly, toward mine.

I grabbed my coat and stepped outside before I could talk myself out of it. The frost crunched under my boots, and the cold air bit at my face. Her car was already backing out of the driveway by the time I reached the edge of my property. I stopped at the fence, watching as her taillights blinked once, twice, then disappeared down the road.

"Should've said something," I muttered under my breath, shoving my hands into my pockets.

The silence that followed her departure was deafening. The chickens clucked in the coop behind me, oblivious to the way my chest tightened. I turned away from the road and headed toward the barn, though I knew I wouldn't be able to focus on work. Not today.

Inside, the familiar scents of hay and earth grounded me, even if my thoughts were a mess. I grabbed a pitchfork and started mucking out the stalls, the repetitive motion giving my hands something to do. But my mind kept wandering. Amberlyn's face when she'd said she'd be back in two weeks. The way she'd looked at me, like she meant it this time. And then the argument, the way her voice had wavered when she said she needed to go back to Boston.

"You have to trust me," she'd said, her eyes searching mine.

I shouldn't have opened my big mouth.

The sound of a truck pulling into the driveway snapped me out of my thoughts. I dropped the pitchfork and stepped outside, half-expecting to see her car. But it was Sawyer's truck, mud spattered along the sides and rust eating away at the tailgate. He climbed out, looking as exhausted as I felt.

"Morning," he said, nodding toward me. "You look awful."

"Thanks. You too." I leaned against the barn door, crossing my arms. "What's up?"

He rubbed the back of his neck, avoiding my gaze. "You got a minute? We need to talk."

I followed him into the house, where he sat heavily at the kitchen table. I grabbed two mugs from the cabinet and poured coffee, sliding one across to him.

"It's about Jen," he started, his voice rough. "She's apparently in town. After the call I got from her lawyer, Jen must've decided to come make my life worse."

I froze, the coffee cup halfway to my lips. "She's here?"

"Yeah. She's at the inn with Maple." He laughed, but it was bitter. "I was dropping her off this morning, and she threw a hissy fit because she wanted to go to see Isla at the bakery. Not her mother. Isla. They've grown so close, but if I lose Maple..."

"You're not going to lose her," I said, setting the cup down. "We'll figure this out."

He shook his head. "I need steady work. Something that looks good on paper. I've been thinking about taking a job with Eastbrook."

"Eastbrook?" My voice came out sharper than I intended. "They're the enemy, though. They're the ones we've been trying to stop from buying up the entire valley."

"I know." He looked up at me, his eyes desperate. "But it's the only offer I've got. And I can't lose my daughter."

"What about Mayor Goldwin?"

"I asked at town hall. There are no positions open. Believe me, Lee, I've tried looking everywhere in town. There's nothing. Nobody's hiring."

I let out a long breath, running a hand through my hair. "There's got to be another way."

"There isn't." He stood, his chair scraping against the floor. "I don't have a choice. It's that or leave again, and I just got home. And Isla... I can't leave her again."

If only Amberlyn had felt the same about me.

"I really am sorry, Levi." He left before I could argue, the door slamming shut behind him.

Chapter Eleven

AMBERLYN

Inside Logan Airport, everything smelled wrong. No wood smoke, no hay, no apples. Just recycled air, someone's overpowering cologne, and burnt coffee from the kiosk near security.

I found a seat at my gate and pulled out my phone. Opened my messages. A few from Kenzie about the video she'd made that'd gone viral on TikTok about the hayride. One from Mom telling me to be safe. And one from Dad saying he missed me already.

That was an hour ago.

I switched to my notes app and stared at the pro/con list I'd been updating since yesterday afternoon when the headhunter called. The cons section now just read: Not Levi. Not home. Not what I want.

But the pros section still had all those practical reasons. Salary. Career advancement. Proving I didn't waste eight years. Financial security for my parents. I could actually help them hang on to the farm if I took the job, using part of the new salary to help them pay their dues.

My fingers hovered over the delete button.

A family walked past. A mom, a dad, and two kids in matching Halloween shirts. The little girl was crying about leaving Grandma's house. Her brother told her they'd come back for Thanksgiving. The mom caught my eye and gave me that exhausted parent smile that said "sorry for the noise."

I smiled back and watched them disappear toward their gate, the little girl still sniffling about Grandma's pumpkin cookies.

Eventually, the flight attendant called for boarding, and I joined the line with my carry-on and this awful feeling that I was walking away from everything that mattered.

Again.

My apartment didn't feel like mine anymore.

Later, I stood in the doorway with my suitcase, staring at the minimalist furniture and the motivational print above the couch that said "Success is a journey, not a destination" in trendy script. When had I bought that? Why had I bought that?

The thermostat was set to sixty-eight, like always, but I was cold. I turned it up to seventy-two. Still cold. Turned it up to seventy-five.

My phone sat on the kitchen counter, silent.

I should unpack. I should shower. I should eat something besides the airport sandwich I'd bought and couldn't finish because it tasted like cardboard.

Instead, I straightened the picture frames on the bookshelf, and then stood in my living room trying to remember what I usually did when I got home from trips.

My phone rang. Not Levi. My boss.

"Hey Julie," I said.

"Amberlyn! You're back, right? Can you possibly swing by the office? Just for an hour. We've got a situation, and it'd be great to have you mediate."

I looked at my suitcase, still by the door. At my apartment that felt like a hotel room. At my phone that Levi wasn't calling.

"Sure. I'll be there in an hour."

"You're a lifesaver. I'll buy you coffee."

She hung up, and I stood there holding my phone, realizing I'd just said yes to work before I'd even unpacked. Before I'd made any decisions about anything. Because this was what I did—I filled the space where feelings should be with tasks and projects and other people's urgent problems.

I grabbed my work bag and headed back out the door.

The office looked exactly the same. Glass walls, open floor plan, a poster about "finding innovative solutions" that I'd walked past every day for three years without really seeing .

My desk was covered in welcome-back sticky notes. Someone had left a plant—a sad little succulent in a pot that said "Don't be a prick."

Julie appeared with coffee. "Okay, so we have a client who wants to shift their entire Q4 campaign to sustainability messaging, but Amanda wrote copy that sounds like an angry teenager, and they hate it, and we need revisions by tomorrow or they're walking."

She shoved a tablet at me.

I took it and scrolled through Amanda's attempt. "DON'T BE TRASH—COMPOST!" and "RECYCLING IS PUNK ROCK."

"Yeah," Julie said. "So if you could just work your magic—"

"Julie." I set down the tablet. "I need to tell you something."

"Tell me after you fix this? Please? I'm begging."

I looked at her stressed face, at my desk covered in sticky notes, at the office full of people I'd worked with for years doing work that suddenly felt completely hollow.

"I'm giving my two weeks' notice on Monday."

Her face went through several expressions before landing on confused. "What? Why? Didn't you just get offered a promotion? Is this about money? Because we can talk about—"

"It's not about money. I'm moving home. My family needs me. My parent's farm is—"

Julie cut me off. "But you're brilliant at this. You've won awards. Clients request you specifically." She sat at the edge of my desk. "You don't just walk away from a career you've built."

"Maybe I built the wrong thing."

Julie studied my face. "You're serious."

"Yeah."

"Okay. But you're not officially starting your notice until Monday, which means you could still change your mind if something better came along. Like that promotion meeting. Definitely go to that meeting."

"I will, but I'm not going to change my mind."

"Just think about it." She stood up. "You've got the weekend. But right now, could you please fix the copy so I don't have a panic attack?"

I looked at the tablet, at the failed copy, at the campaign that needed saving. Three weeks ago I would have been excited about this problem. Would have dove in and solved it and felt accomplished and useful.

Now I just felt tired.

"Two hours," I said. "Then I'm going home."

"Deal."

I spent the next two hours writing copy about composting that somehow made it sound cool without being obnoxious. It was good work. Professional. Exactly what was needed.

It also felt completely meaningless.

When I sent the final draft to Julie, she responded immediately.

> PERFECT. YOU'RE A GENIUS. NEVER
> LEAVE ME.

I stared at those words—never leave me—and thought about Levi. If there was anyone I shouldn't leave, it was him. And I'd done it again.

I grabbed my bag and left before Julie could find another urgent problem for me to solve.

Back at my apartment, I turned the thermostat up to seventy-eight, and I was still cold. My phone showed three texts from Kenzie, one from Isla, and nothing from Levi.

To be fair, I hadn't messaged him either.

I pulled out the peanut butter jar from the cabinet—crunchy, the good kind—and ate three spoonfuls standing in my kitchen. Then I sat on the couch with the jar and my phone and tried to figure out what I was doing.

I decided to respond to my mom's text.

Mom: Call me when you can. Love you.

I hit dial.

"Hi, honey," she answered. "How are you?"

"I'm eating peanut butter straight from the jar in the dark, so you tell me."

"Oh no. What happened?"

I told her about the office, about Julie's reaction, about the job offer still sitting in my inbox. About the argument Levi and I had before I'd left.

"And the terrible part is maybe he's right," I said. "Maybe I should choose this. I've been back six hours, and I've already gone to the office to fix someone else's crisis, and I'm good at it. If I take the promotion, I could help pay off your debts and—"

"It's not your job to pay for your dad and me. You need to decide what is best for you."

"How do I decide what I want?"

She was quiet for a moment, and I heard her moving around—probably in the kitchen, probably making tea because that's what she did when she needed to think.

"Can I tell you what Grandma told me when your dad and I were deciding about the farm?" she finally said.

"Okay," I mumbled around a mouthful of peanut butter.

"She said fear is useful information, but it's terrible at making decisions. She said to listen to what scares you, understand why, and then decide anyway based on what you actually want."

I pulled my knees up to my chest, the peanut butter jar balanced on the armrest. "I'm afraid of both options."

"That's not the answer to what you want."

"I want to come home." The words came out before I could think them through. "I want to save the farm. I want Levi. I want to build something that actually matters instead of writing copy about composting."

"Then that's your answer."

"But what if I'm wrong again? What if I can't save the farm and I prove that I was right to leave in the first place?"

"Then you'll have failed trying to do something you cared about, with people who love you." She paused. "Which is better than succeeding at something that makes you eat peanut butter alone in the dark."

I laughed despite myself. "That's fair."

We talked for a few more minutes—she told me about Kenzie's volleyball game, about Reverand Borris ordering three dozen pumpkins for the church, about Levi being in the barn all day avoiding people. Then she said she loved me and I should get some sleep.

After we hung up, I sat there in my too-warm apartment with my peanut butter jar and my phone and a certainty settling in my chest like something clicking into place.

I opened my laptop and pulled up the job offer email. Director of Marketing. Stock options. Everything I'd told myself I wanted for eight years.

I hit reply and typed: Thank you for this incredible opportunity. After careful consideration, I've decided to pursue a different path. I wish you all the best.

I sent it before I could second-guess myself.

Then I opened my text thread with Levi, and my fingers hovered over the keyboard for a long time. What could I say that I hadn't already said? That I loved him? I'd told him that. That I was coming home? I'd told him that too, and he said he didn't trust me.

Of course, I didn't blame him.

I wouldn't trust me either.

I typed "I turned down the job. I'm coming home for good. Not because I feel guilty. Because it's where I want to be. Because I choose you and the farm and us. I love you."

I stared at the message for a solid minute, then deleted everything and rewrote it:

> We need to talk at the festival on Saturday.
> Please don't give up on us.

I hit send before I could overthink it.

Three dots appeared immediately. My heart jumped into my throat.

Then they disappeared.

Then appeared again.

Then disappeared again.

Finally, after what felt like seventeen years, he responded.

> We should definitely talk when you get back.

That was it. No "I love you." No "I'm so happy you're coming back." Just an agreement that we should talk, which could mean anything.

I set my phone down and picked up the peanut butter jar. Outside my window, Boston hummed with traffic and sirens. Someone's car alarm went off. A couple walked past arguing about whether they'd locked the door.

I missed the quiet. Missed the sound of wind through the oak trees and geese flying overhead and Levi hollering at me over the fence.

My phone buzzed. It wasn't Levi, unfortunately. It was Kenzie.

> MOM TOLD ME. IM SO PROUD OF YOU.
> now please fix things with the boy because
> he's being IMPOSSIBLE and nobody can
> stand to be around him

> also i stole your pink top sorry not sorry

I smiled and set my phone down. Turned off the lights. Sat in the dark in my apartment that had never felt like home, thinking about a pumpkin patch and a boy.

In two days I'd be back there. Walking into the Fall Festival. Facing Levi and whatever "we should talk" meant. It might mean goodbye, which would definitely be awkward after I quit my job and left Boston. It might mean he couldn't forgive me for leaving the first time, couldn't trust me not to leave again, which, again, was completely fair. But then again, it might mean second chances.

Chapter Twelve

LEVI

Sawyer's truck pulled into the driveway around eight on Friday, and he got out moving like someone who'd been awake all night staring at ceiling fans.

"Mediation meeting for custody is during the festival," he said. No greeting, no preamble. "So that's great."

My stomach dropped. "Sawyer—"

"Don't worry. I'm not going with Eastbrook. They didn't want me anyway." He kicked at the gravel. "Mayor Goldwin knows someone in Portland. Design firm needs a project manager. Good salary, benefits, everything I said I'd never do again."

"You'd hate Portland."

"I'd hate losing my daughter more." He looked at me then, and his eyes were red. "So that's probably happening. Leaving after harvest season."

Two people leaving. The thought sat in my chest like a stone. "What about Isla?"

"I think she knows. She's been...distant." He leaned against his truck. "Asher's got drama too. Quinn's ex showed up at the costume shop yesterday. Wanted to 'discuss their relationship' apparently. Asher's been there since last night."

"Is she okay?"

"She's fine. Asher called me at midnight asking if threatening someone counted as assault if you only described in detail what you'd do with your bare hands and a chainsaw."

Despite everything, I almost smiled. "What'd you tell him?"

"That he should maybe not describe anything and definitely call Sheriff Marx." He pushed off the truck. "All three of us are complete disasters right now. You know that?"

"Not a good harvest for the Thatcher boys, it would seem."

"Yeah."

I pulled my grandfather's knife from my pocket, running my thumb along the smooth handle. "I don't know what to say to her if she comes back."

"Start with 'I'm sorry for being an idiot' and see where that goes." He headed toward the barn. "When is she coming back, by the way?"

"Supposed to be today."

"And?"

"Do you see a rental car across the street?"

"If you're going to be crabby, I'm just going to go get what I need and head to the festival," he said, looking at me like I was a petulant child. He really was a good dad.

"Yeah, you should probably go. I'll head down to help set up in a bit," I scratched the back of my neck.

After he left, I stood there with the knife in my hand. Eventually, I sighed and got to work loading my truck for the festival setup.

By noon, the village green was full of people setting up festival booths. I could see the Avery display from my truck—they'd claimed a spot near the gazebo, and even from fifty yards away I could tell Amberlyn wasn't there yet.

The wind picked up as I hammered the last stake into the ground, securing the Thatcher Farms banner to our booth. My fingers had gone numb about twenty minutes ago, but I barely noticed. The sky was the color of wet cement, and the air smelled like rain. I pulled out my phone—40% chance of storms tonight, turning to 90% by midnight. Perfect.

I glanced toward the Avery booth again. Kenzie was there now, wrestling with a tangled string of orange lights while Mrs. Avery arranged pumpkins into a pyramid. Still no Amberlyn.

"You gonna stare at their booth all day or actually help?" Sawyer dropped a crate of apples next to me with a thud.

"I'm working." I grabbed a knife and started slicing samples.

"Uh-huh." He leaned against the table, arms crossed. "Did she text you?"

"Not since she said she was coming back. Which clearly wasn't true." The knife slipped, nicking my thumb. I swore under my breath and stuck the cut in my mouth.

Sawyer exhaled through his nose. "You're a mess."

"Yeah, well." I wiped the blade on my jeans. "Not like you're winning any awards for emotional stability these days."

"Fair." He grabbed an apple and took a loud bite. "But at least I'm not pretending I'm fine."

I didn't respond. The truth was, I wasn't fine. Every time a car pulled into the parking lot, my head snapped up like some kind of pathetic reflex. And every time it wasn't her, the knot in my chest tightened.

Aunt Caroline appeared at the edge of our booth, holding two steaming cups. "Hot cider. Not coffee," she announced, shoving one at me. "Drink it before you turn into an icicle."

I took it, the heat seeping into my stiff fingers. "Thanks."

She gave me a long look, then sighed. "Levi."

"I know."

"Do you?"

I took a sip just to avoid answering. The cider burned all the way down.

Aunt Caroline shook her head. "You boys. Always so determined to suffer in silence." She turned to Sawyer. "And you—stop enabling him."

Sawyer held up his hands. "I'm just here for the free apples."

She muttered something under her breath and marched off toward the bakery contest setup.

The afternoon dragged. I rearranged produce, answered questions about heirloom squash varieties, and pretended not to notice the way people kept glancing between me and the Avery booth. Small towns.

Nothing ever stayed private, even with the tourists, though most of them would come tomorrow for the big day of fall festivities.

By four, the temperature had dropped enough that my breath fogged in the air. The festival officially started tomorrow, but people were already milling around, sampling cider and taking photos of the scarecrow displays.

Still no Amberlyn

The first raindrop hit my neck.

"Hey, some of the others are saying to call it a day," Sawyer said, gesturing towards a few other booths. I say we pack it up. Rain's coming early."

We worked in silence, loading what we could into the truck and covering the rest with tarps. Around us, other vendors did the same, scrambling to protect their booths before the storm hit.

By the time we finished, the rain was coming down in sheets. I climbed into the driver's seat, soaked and shivering.

Sawyer turned the heat full blast. "She's coming back, Lee."

"Maybe." I stared through the windshield at the blur of rain. "Maybe not."

He didn't answer. There wasn't anything to say.

I started the truck and pulled out of the parking lot, the wipers fighting a losing battle against the downpour. The storm had arrived.

Amberlyn hadn't.

The storm woke me up in the middle of the night. It howled outside, rattling the windows of the farmhouse as if it was trying to get in. I jolted awake, the sound of rain pounding the roof and wind whipping through the trees pulling me from sleep. My first thought was the farm. The animals. The crops.

I yanked on my boots, not bothering with socks, and grabbed a rain-coat from the hook by the door. The coat was more of a formality—I'd be soaked in seconds anyway. The moment I stepped outside, the rain hit me like a wall. The wind nearly knocked me sideways as I fought my way toward the barn.

The goats were restless, huddled together in their pen, their bleats barely audible over the storm. I checked the latch on the barn doors, making sure they were secure. The roof groaned under the weight of the rain, but it held. For now. I moved to the greenhouse next, cursing under my breath as I saw water pooling near the base. I grabbed a shovel and dug a trench to divert the water, the mud sucking at my boots with every step.

By the time I made it back to the house, I was dripping, my clothes clinging to me like a second skin. I kicked off my boots and peeled off the soaked raincoat, leaving it in a heap by the door. I'd deal with it in the morning. Maybe. Maybe not.

I stumbled into the kitchen, water dripping from my hair and pooling on the floor. My phone lay on the counter, the screen lit up with a barrage of notifications. Missed calls. Texts. I swiped it open, my fingers still damp and clumsy.

Frank Avery had called twice and left a message.

> Hey, Levi. Power's out over here too. You good on generators?

Aunt Caroline's message was brief.

> Made it home from the cafe safe. Stay dry.

Then there was Amberlyn. Her name on the screen made my chest tighten. I scrolled through her messages, a knot in my chest tightening with each one until it was difficult to breathe.

> Levi, I'm so sorry. I missed my connecting flight because of the storm. The weather's insane. I can't get through to anyone. My parents won't pick up. Unfortunately, I don't think there are any flights until tomorrow afternoon. Not sure what to do.

> I rented a car. I'll drive the rest of the way to Acorn Field Heights and be there for the festival tomorrow (albeit a bit sleepy). Excited to see you!

> Don't freak out, but I'm stuck. I tried to drive, but the storm is really bad, and now I'm off the road. I called a tow truck, but the guy said it's going to take hours. I wasn't the first to call. I don't think I'm going to make it in time. I'm so sorry.

The last one came in ten minutes ago.

> Do you think I should try walking to the closest town? I think there was one a few miles back. I don't know what to do. My parents and Kenzie still aren't answering any of my calls. Could you please call me. I know you're upset I left, but—

I didn't think. I just hit the call button, pressing the phone to my ear as it rang. It took three tries before she answered.

"Levi?" Her voice was shaky, almost swallowed by the sound of rain pounding on her end. "Oh, thank goodness. I was starting to think—"

"Where are you?"

"I—I don't know. Some back road. The GPS stopped working and I was trying to get it fixed. There must be cell towers down. I think I'm about an hour from the highway, but I couldn't see the road. I just—I slid off into the ditch. I'm sorry, I'm so sorry. I didn't want to miss the festival. I didn't want to miss you."

"Are you hurt?"

"No. Just... stuck. The car's fine, I think. But I can't move it. The tow truck said it'll be hours before they can get here. I thought I could maybe walk to the last town I passed through, but—"

"That's an awful idea." I was already grabbing my keys and stampeding towards the front door.

"Well, I don't know what else to do."

The door slammed behind me, and rain pelted my face. "Stay in the car. Keep the doors locked. I'm coming to get you."

"Levi, it's the middle of the night. It's pouring. You can't—"

"Send me your location." I shifted my phone to my other ear as I unlocked my truck and wrenched the door open. Rain fell in sheets off the hood, and by the time I slid into the driver's seat, my clothes were re-soaked.

"Alright, I sent it. Did you get it?"

I glanced down at my phone and opened the latest text, mapping the gps with a second click. "Yeah. Stay safe. I'll be there in three hours. Maybe more if the rain doesn't let up."

"Levi, you don't have to—"

The engine roared to life, and I shoved it into gear, not caring that the wipers could barely keep up with the rain.

"I'm coming. Just stay put."

Before she could argue, I hung up, dropping my phone into my cup holder. With the storm still raging, I'd need all my focus on driving. The road out of Acorn Field Valley was dark, the headlights cutting through the downpour in narrow beams. My hands clenched the wheel, knuckles white, as I pushed the truck harder than I probably should have. Every time my wheels skidded over the road, I held my breath until they made contact again. About halfway out of town, I realized that in my rush to leave, I'd completely forgotten socks and boots. Dumb move, but I wasn't going back.

The storm didn't let up. The rain came in waves, slamming into the windshield in bursts that made it hard to see. I kept the radio off, the only sound the steady thrum of the engine and the endless hammer of rain. My mind raced, jumping between the image of Amberlyn sitting alone in her car, scared and stranded, and all the things that could've been worse. Very happy thoughts that definitely didn't make me toe the gas pedal more than I probably should've.

The highway was emptier than usual, but the rain made it treacherous. I passed three cars pulled over, hazard lights flashing, and one spun out in the ditch. My stomach twisted with each one. I prayed over and over again that she'd be alright.

When my phone alerted me to turn onto a back road towards her location, I nearly missed my exit. It was a narrow dirt road, the kind that didn't get plowed in winter. The truck's tires churned through the mud as I followed the map's faint blue line.

And then, finally, after three and a half hours of white-knuckle driving, I saw it. The faint glow of headlights off to the side of the road. Amberlyn's car was tilted at an angle, half-hidden by the tall grass at the edge of a field. I pulled up behind it, my headlights illuminating everything. The rain was still coming down, but I barely noticed as I jumped out and ran barefoot to her car.

She was sitting in the driver's seat, her face pale in the dim light. When she saw me, her eyes widened, and she scrambled to open the door. It swung open, and she launched herself at me, her arms wrapping around my neck.

"You came," she murmured into my shoulder, her voice muffled by the rain and the steady thrum of the storm.

I held onto her, one hand gripping her waist, the other brushing her wet hair out of her face. "Of course I came. Now let's get you out of here," I said, guiding her toward the truck. The rain soaked through us both, but it didn't matter. Not anymore. She was here. She was safe. And for the first time since she left, I felt like I could breathe.

"Where are your boots?"

Chapter Thirteen

AMBERLYN

I couldn't stop my hands from shaking. Not from cold, though the heater was blasting air that barely touched the chill in my bones. From adrenaline crash, from exhaustion, from the reality that Levi had driven three and a half hours barefoot through a storm to get me.

I checked my phone even though it had lost charge ten minutes into the drive. And thanks to Levi's aversion to iPhones and my stupidity in not bringing a charging cable, it was going to stay that way until we got back.

"You can relax," Levi said, eyes on the road. "We're safe."

"I know." I set the phone down, then picked it up again. Adjusted the air vent so it wasn't blowing directly on my face. Adjusted it back. "I just—thank you. For coming."

"You said that already."

"I know. I'm saying it again."

His jaw was tight, hands white-knuckled on the wheel even though the rain was letting up. He looked exhausted—hair plastered to his forehead, jacket soaked through, shadows under his eyes that hadn't been there the last time I'd seen him.

We drove in silence, and I watched the windshield wipers beat their rhythm while my brain spun through everything I needed to say. How to explain what I did in Boston. How to prove I meant it this time. How to—

"Just say it," he said.

"What?"

"Whatever you're overthinking. Just say it."

I made myself look at him. "Are you mad at me?"

"For getting stuck?"

"For leaving. For going back to Boston. After everything we said."

His hands tightened on the wheel. For a long moment, he didn't answer, just checked the rearview mirror twice even though the road behind us was empty.

"Yeah," he said finally. "I was mad. And hurt. And—" He stopped, shook his head. "What happened in Boston?"

"My company offered me a promotion. Director of Marketing. Huge salary, corner office, everything I've been working toward for eight years." I pulled out my phone, put it down, picked it up again. "She said I'd be throwing my career away. That I was too talented to waste on a failing farm."

Levi's jaw clenched, but he stayed quiet.

"I told my boss thanks, but no."

"Just like that?"

"Just like that. Right there in the meeting." I was talking faster now, trying to make him understand. "I turned in my resignation. Broke my lease. Started packing my apartment. I was done the moment I left Acorn Field Heights. I just had to make it official."

"And then?"

"And then I drove straight to the airport to catch my flight back. But the storm cancelled everything and I missed my connection and—" My throat went tight. I swallowed hard. "I couldn't miss the festival. Couldn't miss you. And then I ended up in a ditch and—"

"Hey." He glanced at me. "You're here. That's what matters."

"I know, but—"

"You came back." His voice was careful, measured. "That's what matters."

I wanted to grab onto that, to let it be enough. But there was something in his tone that wasn't quite convincing. Something held back.

"Do you believe me?" I asked. "About staying?"

He was quiet for so long I thought he wouldn't answer. "I want to," he eventually said in a voice that was barely loud enough over the sound of the heat blasting and the windshield wipers swiping back and forth.

"But you don't."

"I'm trying to." He checked the mirror again. "You turned down your dream job. Packed your apartment. Drove through a storm. Those aren't small things. I know that. But—"

"But I've failed you before."

"It's not..." he sighed and bit his cheek. "Yeah."

We drove in silence, and I didn't know what else to say. How to prove something that could only be proven over time. I pulled out my phone again, checked it even though I knew I'd only get a black screen, and shoved it back in my pocket.

The sky was starting to lighten ahead of us—not quite dawn, but close. Maybe an hour from home.

Levi reached over and took my hand.

I looked at him, surprised.

"I'm scared," he said, eyes still on the road. "That you'll wake up and realize this was a mistake. That small-town life isn't enough. That I'm not enough." His thumb traced circles on my palm. "But I'm going to try to believe you anyway. We'll save your family's farm now that you're back."

His phone buzzed in the cupholder. Then again. And again. A cascade of notifications all arriving at once.

"They're all from Sawyer," I said, reaching for it. "Want me to look?"

"Please."

The screen was full of missed calls and texts—all from his brother. My stomach dropped.

I scrolled through, and the messages made my throat tight. "Maple's missing."

His knuckles went white. "What?"

Before I could read him any of the texts, the phone rang again. I answered and put it on speaker.

"Lee?" Sawyer's voice was wrecked. "Finally. Cell tower went down,

I couldn't reach anyone—Maple's gone. She ran away from Jen. I've been looking for three hours and I can't find her anywhere, and with the storm—"

"Hey, take a deep breath." Levi's voice went calm, steady, the way it did when animals were spooked. "Where have you looked?"

"Everywhere. The house, the barn, the fields. Jen said they fought about going home and Maple just ran into the storm three hours ago. She's five and she's been out there for three hours—"

"Have you checked the bakery?"

A pause. "The bakery?"

"Isla's place. You guys have been spending a lot of time there. Maple talks about it constantly."

"I—no. I didn't even think—" Hope crept into his voice. "I'm maybe ten minutes out."

"We're ninety minutes away. We'll help when we get there." Levi's voice was still calm, but I could see tension in every line of his body. "Call the second you know anything."

"Tower's still spotty but I'll try. Thank you—"

The line went dead.

Levi pressed harder on the gas. Not reckless, but faster. The speedometer crept up.

"She's okay," I said, even though I had no way to know. "Sawyer will find her."

"She's five." His voice was tight. "Anything could have happened."

"But you're right about the bakery. That's exactly where she'd go, right? She and Isla have gotten close over the last couple weeks. I'm sure that's where she went."

He didn't answer, just drove, and I kept my hand on his arm because I didn't know what else to do.

The rest of the drive passed in silence broken only by the sound of tires on wet pavement. Dawn broke, and the storm finally cleared. The roads were slick, littered with branches and a few downed trees, which Levi stopped to remove when possible.

When we finally turned onto the road to Millstone road, something in my chest unclenched. Almost home.

Levi pulled up to my parents' farmhouse, and before the truck was even fully stopped, my mom was running out in her bathrobe.

"Oh, thank goodness!" She pulled me into a hug so tight I could barely breathe. "We got your texts, but couldn't reach you, the storm was so bad, we thought—"

"I'm fine. I'm sorry." I hugged her back, breathing in the smell of her laundry detergent and coffee. "My phone died. I tried calling you."

My dad appeared behind my mom, looking exhausted. He nodded at Levi. "Thank you for bringing her home."

"Of course."

Kenzie burst out the door, still in pajamas, her hair a mess. "Oh my goodness, you're alive! We've been freaking out all night!" She threw her arms around me.

"I'm fine."

Levi's phone rang. Sawyer.

We all froze.

He answered. "Did you find her?"

I couldn't hear the response, but I watched his shoulders drop, tension bleeding out.

"She's okay?" A pause. "I knew it." Another pause, and something complicated crossed his face. "All night?" He listened. "Yeah. Okay. Give her a hug from me, and let me know how the custody meeting goes today. Yeah. Love you too."

He hung up and looked at all of us. "Maple's safe. Was hiding at Isla's bakery the whole time. She's fine."

Relief hit so hard I had to lean against the truck. Kenzie made a small sound, and my mom put her hand over her heart.

"Maple was missing?" My mom asked, her eyes wide. "Oh, poor Sawyer. I'm sure he had a long night too."

"Thank goodness he found her," my dad said.

"Yeah. Jen's trying to get full custody. The meeting is today." Levi looked at me. "Look, I should go. Check my farm for damage. I'll see you at the festival?"

"I'll be there."

He unloaded my suitcases from the back seat of his truck before he climbed back in and drove away. I watched him cross Millstone and pull all the way up his driveway, where he parked next to the barn.

"Come inside," my mom said, wrapping an arm around my waist and tugging me towards the house. "You need dry clothes and sleep."

But sleep felt impossible. I was too wired, too full of everything that had just happened. I changed into dry clothes and lay down, but after staring at the ceiling for twenty minutes, I gave up and went back downstairs.

My dad was in the kitchen with coffee, looking at his laptop.

"Couldn't sleep either?" I asked.

"Storm did a number on the festival setup from what Mayor Goldwin said." He gestured at the screen. "They're trying to figure out if they can still open."

I poured coffee with shaking hands—exhaustion making me clumsy. "The whole town will help. We'll make it work."

He was quiet for a moment, not looking at me.

"What?" I asked.

"Eastbrook called while you were gone." He still wouldn't meet my eyes. "Made another offer. Higher. They'll pay off all our debts and give us enough to retire and pay for Kenzie's college."

My coffee cup stopped halfway to my mouth. "What did you tell them?"

"That your mother and I need to discuss it." He finally looked at me, and he looked old suddenly. Tired. "We've been farming this land for four generations, Amberlyn. But the debts keep piling up. Equipment keeps breaking. We're not getting younger."

"So you're still considering selling." It wasn't a question.

"The business you've helped bring in paid off the most important bills, but we're considering our options."

I set my coffee down before I dropped it. My hands found the salt and pepper shakers, straightening them even though they were already straight. "Even though I choose to stay? To help?"

"I know you want to save this place. I love that you do." He reached across and covered my hand with his, stopping my compulsive straightening. "But sometimes saving something means knowing when to let go."

The words made my eyes burn. I pulled my hand back and stood up, needing to move, to do something. "We should talk about this when I'm not—when I've slept."

"Of course." He stood too, kissed my forehead. "Get some rest. We'll figure it out."

But as I stood there alone in the kitchen with cold coffee and my dad's words echoing, I couldn't shake the feeling that maybe we wouldn't figure it out. Maybe choosing to stay wasn't enough. Maybe I was eight years too late.

I looked out the window at the pumpkin patch, golden in the early morning light. Four generations of Averys had worked this land. I'd done the research for the history lesson I'd given during the hayride. I knew the historical significance of the place. Unfortunately, it likely wouldn't matter in the end. In fact, I might be home just in time to watch my home get sold to developers who'd turn it into condos or a shopping center or whatever made them the most profit.

Chapter Fourteen

LEVI

At five-thirty I gave up trying to get anywhere near sleep and headed to the village green. The storm had turned weeks of work into wreckage—tents twisted like metal sculptures, booths smashed to splinters, decorations blown three blocks away. Pumpkins everywhere, most of them destroyed.

Mayor Goldwin was already there with coffee and his clipboard, surveying the damage.

"Morning, Levi. Your place okay?"

"Minor damage. Yours?"

"Tree through the garage." He handed me coffee. "Your aunt's booth is bad. She's over there now. You might want to start there."

I found Aunt Caroline surrounded by broken tables and shattered equipment. She wasn't crying, but her mouth was set in that tight line that meant she was close.

"I'll help rebuild it," I said.

"I figured you would. That's why I'm not going to shed any tears over it."

I started sorting debris. "Where's Asher?"

"Helping Quinn board up the broken windows at her shop. He said he'd come help your booth after."

We worked in silence, pulling apart what couldn't be saved. The sun broke through the clouds, turning everything the color of honey. Leaves scattered across the green like someone had dumped out bags of them. The air smelled like wet earth and sawdust.

Asher showed up around six-thirty with lumber and tools, looking as exhausted as I felt.

"Quinn okay?" I asked.

"Shop's damaged but fixable. It caught on fire last night when lightning struck it. Doesn't help that her ex showed up during the storm." His jaw tightened. "I convinced him to leave."

"Convinced how?"

"Politely. While holding a hammer."

I snorted, rolling my eyes. "Just don't say anything to the sheriff."

"Wouldn't dream of it."

We spent two hours building Aunt Caroline a new booth from scratch. My hands shook from exhaustion, and I hammered my thumb twice—something I hadn't done in a very long time. By the time we finished, the booth looked better than before, and my aunt was crying for real now.

"Thank you," she said. "Both of you."

"That's what family does," Asher said. He checked his watch. "I'm going back to Quinn's. Make sure she's really okay. I'll help with the Thatcher booth later, Lee. Let me know if you hear from Sawyer about the custody meeting."

After he left, I walked to where my booth used to be. Like Aunt Caroline's, it was destroyed. I was standing there trying to figure out where to start when I heard her voice.

"It looks worse than it is."

I turned. Amberlyn was walking toward me with her whole family. They all looked exhausted, but they'd shown up anyway.

"That's a lie," I said.

"Okay, yes. It's terrible." She stopped close enough that I could see the circles under her eyes. "We just finished with ours. Thought we might help with yours."

"That's nice, but I don't need—"

"Take it from someone too stubborn to accept help, and accept the help," Frank said, clapping me on the shoulder. "I know you've been fixing up our place when you thought no one was watching."

"Dolores?" I asked, raising an eyebrow.

"Dolores," he confirmed with a grin. "I want to thank you, Levi. And I want to help with this booth."

"Mr. Avery—"

"You didn't give me a choice when you fixed my fence, so I'm not going to give you a choice with this." He squeezed my shoulder and started to pick through the wreckage.

"It's about time someone helped you the way you've been helping everyone else," Amberlyn's mom said, patting me on the cheek before joining her husband.

"Besides, my sister likes you and draws little hearts around your name when she thinks no one is watching." Kenzie ducked out of reach as Amberlyn tried to smack her in the arm, giggling as she moved towards where my banner had blown against a tree.

Amberlyn rolled her eyes, then walked over to me. "I told them to be cool, and that's apparently not in their vocabulary." She nudged me with her shoulder. "But they're right. You've been working so hard to keep this valley intact. You're the hero of this town."

"That's ridiculous."

"Well, after last night and all the things you've been doing for my family, you're my hero."

I blinked at Amberlyn, unsure what to do with the words "my hero." The morning sun caught the gold in her chestnut hair, and I noticed the way she bit her bottom lip.

"Yeah well," I rubbed the back of my neck, "anyone would've come to get you in that storm."

She snorted. "No, they wouldn't have. Not through those roads, not after dark."

Her parents were laughing at something Kenzie said while they pried apart broken signage. The sight of them rebuilding my booth made my throat tight.

Amberlyn nudged me again. "Come on. Where do we start?"

I exhaled. "Pallets first. Then we can salvage what's left of the signage."

We worked in comfortable silence, the kind I remembered from when we used to work together in high school. The Averys moved around me; Frank re-stacking the unbroken crates, Kenzie complaining about splinters, Amelia humming while she swept up glass.

Amberlyn stayed beside me the entire time.

Kenzie eventually tossed a crumpled banner at us. "You two realize everyone can see you making heart eyes at each other, right?"

Amberlyn threw a handful of wood shavings at her just as a man in a navy business suit walked up.

The man wore polished dress shoes as he stepped around the soggy wreckage. He surveyed my ruined booth before turning to me.

"Quite the storm," he said with a friendly smile.

"Yeah," I said. My gaze flicked to Amberlyn, who straightened up from sorting pumpkins, muddy hands braced on her hips.

"If I remember correctly, you're Levi Thatcher and Amberlyn Avery, right?" The man asked, surveying the collapsed tent beside my booth. He extended a hand toward me without seeming to register the grime coating mine. "Collin Hallesbee."

The name didn't mean anything to me, but something about his easy demeanor did. Amberlyn stepped closer as Collin shook her hand too.

"That's us," Amberlyn said, returning his smile. "How can we help you, Mr. Hallesbee?"

"Actually, I'm here to help you. Both of you. I'm sure you don't remember me, but I was here for the hayride with my family."

Hayride. That's where I'd seen him.

"You had two boys, and your wife was asking about the buildings on the outskirts of my parents' property," Amberlyn said, snapping her fingers. "I remember you."

Collin grinned. "Excellent, and yes, my wife is quite a history nerd." He reached into his breast pocket and pulled out a business card—East River Agritourism stamped in minimalist green letters. "I run a small agricultural tourism company. Mostly educational programs, sustainable farming showcases. We work with a lot of schools across the state." His gaze bounced between Amberlyn and me. "And I'd like to partner with both of your farms."

Amberlyn stilled beside me. Frank stopped hammering behind us.

Collin scratched his jaw, oblivious or politely ignoring the sudden tension. "We've been looking to expand into this valley. Authenticity's hard to come by in most commercial farms, but yours?" He gestured toward the Averys' rebuilt booth down the green. "You've got the real deal. Families and teachers want this experience—collecting eggs, pressing cider, candle-making—but it's gotta be hands-on."

"And profitable?" Frank asked bluntly, coming to stand behind Amberlyn. He took off his work glove and held out his hand. "Frank Avery, Amberlyn's dad."

Collin blinked and then returned his smile. "Extremely. Pleasure to meet you, Mr. Avery. I'm sure you and Mr. Thatcher are busy today and tomorrow with the festival, but if you have time on Monday, I'd love to sit down and talk numbers, guest capacity, seasonal tours, partnerships, you know, the works."

Amberlyn turned her face toward me, mouthing *Holy Cow*.

"—initial investment covers repairs," Collin was saying. "We'd market online, staff occasionally during peak seasons—your teams still run operations." He glanced at Frank and me. "It'd be enough to wipe out debts. Not a buyout, just..."

"A lifeline," Amelia Avery murmured, weaving her fingers in with her husband's.

Collin hesitated when none of us spoke. "Too fast?"

Frank chuckled and shook his head. "I've heard worse offers."

Amberlyn exhaled sharply. "This would keep both farms open?"

Collin nodded. "If you want it. My wife is also part of the historical society, and is interested in doing some more research into the buildings on the edge of your property. She wants to see if she can get them registered as historical buildings."

I was pretty sure Amberlyn's mom was about to cry. "That would be incredible."

I studied Collin. No Eastbrook slickness, no evil glint. Just a guy who'd sat through Amberlyn's history lessons and decided it was worth paying for.

Kenzie whistled as she joined me on my other side. "You're telling me we don't have to sell?"

Collin frowned. "Was that on the table?"

Frank clapped him on the shoulder, steering him toward my salvaged pallets like they'd known each other for years. "Why wait until Monday? Let's talk details."

"But I'd like to partner with Mr. Thatcher's farm too and—"

"I'll talk to you on Monday, Mr. Hallesbee," I said, giving him a brief nod.

Amberlyn stayed rooted beside me, her pinkie brushing mine as her father led Collin to Aunt Caroline's repaired booth.

"I think," she drawled, "we might pull this off."

I curled my pinky around hers.

"Yeah," I said. "We might."

Chapter Fifteen

AMBERLYN

The festival was a success. Families wandered between booths with cider and caramel apples, children ran around in costumes and darted between hay bales. The smell of wood smoke and pumpkin spice and fried dough mixed with the cooler evening air. The sound of fiddle music came from the main stage and laughter and conversations layered over each other.

I was helping my mom at the Avery booth when Levi appeared, looking tired but content. We'd barely talked since the festival opened—both of us too busy with our own booths, our own families, the steady stream of visitors who kept asking questions and buying things and taking photos.

"Hey," he said.

"Hey yourself." I handed my mom the cash box. "Need help with your booth?"

"Already packed up for the night. Asher's loading my truck with leftover produce." He shoved his hands into his pockets. "Walk with me?"

My mom made a shooing motion. "Go. We've got this."

We walked through the festival as it wound down for the first night, past vendors closing down displays and families heading to their cars.

The sky was shifting from gold to pink, the temperature dropping enough that I could see our breath. They'd all come back tomorrow though for the final day of the festival.

Levi led me toward the edge of the green to an empty bench. We sat down, surrounded by fallen leaves the color of fire. The festival noise was distant here, just a pleasant hum under the sound of wind through branches.

"I'm so glad you came back in time for the festival, Amberlyn. But..." He sighed and bit his cheek. "I don't want to hold you back. If you need to go back to Boston, if you need to take that job, if you need—"

"I'm not going back to Boston."

"But what if you wake up and regret this? Regret staying, regret choosing a small town over a career, regret—" He stopped, his jaw tight. "Regret me."

"Hey." I waited until he looked at me. "I will not regret you. I have already spent eight years regretting leaving you. I'm not doing that again."

"But what if—"

"No what-ifs. Only right nows. I can't promise I'll never have doubts or hard days or moments where I wonder what my life would have looked like if I'd made different choices." I pulled out my phone, opened my notes app. "But look at this."

I showed him the list I'd been building since dawn—ideas for the farm partnership, marketing strategies, educational program concepts, seasonal event plans. Pages of notes about building something permanent.

"These aren't pro/con lists about staying or leaving," I said. "They're plans. Proper plans for building something here. With you. With my family. With this community."

He scrolled through the notes, and something in his face shifted. "This is detailed."

"I couldn't sleep, so I might have gotten a little obsessive about farm cooperative strategies and agritourism marketing and sustainable agricultural education programs." I took my phone back. "The point is, I'm not keeping one foot out the door anymore. I'm all in. Both feet planted. Probably building an entire house while I'm at it because apparently I can't do anything halfway."

"That sounds exhausting."

"It probably will be. But it's a good kind of exhausting. The kind that comes from building something instead of running away from things." I straightened a fallen leaf on the ground. "You don't hold me back, Levi. You make me better. You make me want to be someone who shows up and stays and builds things that last. Do you think you could ever forgive me for leaving? Could ever trust me again?"

He was quiet for a long moment, just looking at me like he was trying to decide if this was real. If I were real. If any of this could actually work.

"I love you," he said finally. "I've loved you since we were kids carving initials into the oak tree on our property line. I loved you when you left. I loved you every day you were gone. And I love you now." His hand found mine. "And I'm choosing to believe you're staying. Even though I'm still scared. Even though I don't know how this ends. I'm choosing to trust you anyway."

"Good." I squeezed his hand. "Because I love you too. And I'm staying. And we're going to build something amazing together. It's going to be hard and complicated and sometimes we'll want to quit, but we're not going to. Because we're stubborn and we're finally on the same page and we're done wasting time."

Levi kissed me. The moment his lips touched mine, everything else fell away—the fading music, the crisp night air, the earthy scent of fallen leaves. His kiss was gentle but certain, like he'd been waiting all day to do just this. The scratch of his work-roughened thumb traced my cheekbone, anchoring me here.

When he pulled back, his exhale warmed my skin, his eyes searching mine for hesitation that wasn't there.

"I love you, and I'd like to do this all night. But we should get back," I said. "Mayor Goldwin's doing closing remarks."

"Unfortunately, I think you're right."

We walked back to the festival holding hands, and nothing in the world could wipe the grin from my face.

Mayor Goldwin was on the main stage when we arrived. "Thank

you all for making this year's Fall Festival a success! Despite some weather challenges—" everyone laughed "—we came together as a community and made it happen. That's what Acorn Field Heights does. We show up for each other."

Applause and cheers. I spotted my family near their booth—my parents holding hands, Kenzie with her friends.

Levi's hand tightened on mine. Across the crowd, I saw Sawyer with Maple on his shoulders, and Isla standing next to Sawyer, grinning up at Maple. Asher stood with his arm around Quinn, whispering something in her ear.

Later, we sat on Levi's porch with cider and watched the moon rise over the pumpkin fields. The air was cold enough now that we needed blankets, and the stars were coming out one by one in a sky so clear it felt infinite.

"Next year," I said, "we should do the hayride earlier in the season. Get more families with young kids before it gets too cold."

"Already thinking about next year?"

"I'm already thinking about the next ten years." I pulled out my phone, opened a new note. "We could switch up the corn maze too, maybe add a specific night where it's a scarefest and have people dress up and chase the tourists with chainsaws. Oh, and maybe we could partner with the elementary school—"

"It's almost midnight," Levi said. "Maybe we could plan the future tomorrow."

"But I have ideas."

"You always have ideas." He took my phone and set it down. "Right now, let's just sit here and be happy we made it through the last twenty-four hours."

"Okay, but don't let me forget to tell you about my idea for a jack-o'-lantern hunt. Oh, and the haunted barn tour. And did I tell you about the chili cook-off idea I had?"

I'm pretty sure he kissed me to shut me up.

I didn't complain.

Read the First Chapter in Sawyer and Isla's Book

Chapter 1

SAWYER

Five-year-olds have zero respect for carefully laid plans. One second, Maple, my daughter, was holding my hand as we walked past Sugar & Spice Bakery—the establishment I'd been avoiding for two solid months—and the next, she yanked free and bolted straight for the green-awninged storefront like it was made of candy and wishes and unicorn sparkles.

"Maple!" The word came out strangled. I lunged after her, but she had the advantage of small size and complete lack of self-preservation instincts as she ran across the street. Thank goodness for small towns with little traffic. The bakery door swung open, the bell chiming with cheerful obliviousness, and my daughter disappeared inside.

I stood on the sidewalk for half a second, weighing my options. Let her go in alone and potentially get kidnapped by a pastry chef? Follow her and face the woman whose heart I broke seven years ago? Both options were terrible. But only one involved potential kidnapping, so I pushed through the door and immediately regretted the choice right away.

The bakery smelled like cinnamon and fresh bread, warm and sweet and so painfully familiar my chest tightened. I'd forgotten this smell, or maybe I'd tried to forget it. Isla always talked about opening a bakery that smelled like happiness, back when we were seventeen and stupid enough to make plans. Turned out she'd done it without me.

The interior was bigger than it looked from the outside. Display cases lined the left wall, full of pastries shaped like pumpkins and ghosts and things that probably tasted like heaven. Small tables with mismatched chairs filled the right side, each one decorated with a mason jar holding orange mums. Everything was exactly the kind of place Isla would create. Warm and welcoming and just different enough to be interesting.

And there, behind the counter, pulling a tray of something golden from the oven, was Isla Mercado herself.

Two months. I'd managed two months of careful route-planning and strategic timing to avoid this exact moment. Two months of taking the long way around town, of grocery shopping at odd hours, of becoming the person who checked parking lots before getting out of his truck. All of it, wasted because my daughter really wanted a cookie.

Isla hadn't noticed us yet. She hummed under her breath while she worked, some song I didn't recognize, her blonde braid swinging as she moved. She wore a white apron covered in flour handprints and had a smudge of what looked like chocolate on her cheek. Seven years, and she still did that thing where she got completely absorbed in what she was doing, the rest of the world fading away.

Some things you don't forget, no matter how hard you try.

"Are you the cookie princess?" Maple's voice rang out across the bakery, loud and delighted and completely oblivious to the fact that she'd just destroyed my life. "Because this place smells like magic, and only princesses make magic cookies!"

Isla turned around. Her gaze landed on Maple first, and her expression softened into something warm and genuine and completely unguarded.

Then she looked up and saw me standing in the doorway like a coward, and every bit of warmth drained from her face.

For three seconds, nobody moved. The oven timer beeped. Somewhere in the back room, someone was hammering something. Outside, a car honked. But inside the bakery, time did this weird stuttering thing where I could see every expression that crossed Isla's face—surprise, recognition, hurt, anger, and then finally, nothing. Her features went blank, smooth like a mask sliding into place.

"Sawyer." She said my name like it was a diagnosis. Like she was confirming something unfortunate but entirely expected.

My throat was too dry. I swallowed twice before managing, "Hi."

Brilliant. Seven years of imagined conversations, and the best I could manage was "hi." My seventeen-year-old self would be ashamed. My current self was too busy trying not to bolt back out the door.

Maple tugged on my hand, bouncing on her toes. "Daddy, you look the cookie princess is real! Doesn't she look like a princess?"

Isla's gaze dropped back to Maple, and something shifted in her expression. She wiped her hands on her apron and moved toward the display case. "Cookie princess is a new one. Most people just call me Isla." She glanced at Maple, then back at me, and I watched her do the math. Five-year-old kid. My kid, obviously. Which meant—

Her jaw tightened. There it was. The moment she put together that I'd moved on, had a whole life after I left, while she was here building her bakery alone.

Except that wasn't the entire story, and I couldn't exactly explain it in front of Maple, so I stood there like an idiot while my daughter charmed the one person in town who had every reason to hate me.

"I'm Maple, and I'm almost six, and I really, really love your bakery." Maple pressed her face against the display case glass, leaving a small nose print. "It smells happy."

The corner of Isla's mouth twitched. Not quite a smile, but close enough that something in my chest did a painful flip. "It does, doesn't it?" She pulled out a pumpkin cookie decorated with a jack-o'-lantern face and placed it on a small plate. "That's the cinnamon. It's a happiness spice."

She handed the plate to Maple, and for a second our fingers almost touched as I reached out reflexively to help. We both jerked back as if we'd been burned.

Maple didn't notice. She was already cradling her cookie like it were made of gold, examining the jack-o'-lantern face. "This is the most beautiful cookie in the whole entire world. Can I eat it, or should we frame it?"

"You can eat it," Isla said. Her voice had that warm, patient tone she always used to use when explaining things, back when we were kids ourselves. "That's what cookies are for."

"My daddy said we couldn't come in here."

"I'm sure he did." Isla's gaze flicked to me. "Welcome back to town, by the way, Sawyer. I'd say it's good to see you, but we both know I'd be lying."

I deserved them. I deserved worse.

"How much for the cookie?"

Isla opened her mouth, but paused when Maggie did a little happy dance. A small smile broke across Isla's lips, and she sighed. "Don't worry about it."

"Really, I don't mind paying, and—"

From the back room, the hammering stopped. My youngest brother's voice called out, "Isla, where'd you want these shelves? The measurements aren't—" Asher appeared in the doorway, saw me, and stopped dead. "Oh. Sawyer. You're... here."

"And you're here. We were just leaving," I said, at the same time Maple said, "Can I sit at that table? Please? I don't want to drop crumbs on the floor because that would be rude, and Daddy says we're always polite to princesses."

Isla and I both opened our mouths. She got there first. "You can sit wherever you want."

Maple made a beeline for the table nearest the window, the one with the clearest view of the street and the pumpkin-shaped salt and pepper shakers. She settled into the chair, swinging her legs, and took the tiniest, most delicate bite of her cookie. Her eyes went wide.

"Daddy, this is the best cookie I've ever had. I'm going to marry this cookie."

"Pretty sure that's not legal, jellybean."

"Then you have to marry to princess who made it so I can have cookies all day." She looked at Isla with absolute seriousness. "Will you marry my daddy? He's very responsible. He makes my bed almost every day."

Isla's eyes went wide. "Oh, that's... wow. I think the better option is for you to come here when you need a little sugar."

I pulled out the chair across from Maple and sat, because standing in the middle of the bakery while my daughter proposed I marry my ex-girlfriend was far too awkward.

"Yikes..." Asher cleared his throat. "I should get back to—yeah." He disappeared into the back room without finishing the sentence, which was the smartest choice anyone had made all morning.

Isla turned back to her work, dismissing us. She moved around the kitchen area, pulling trays, checking temperatures, doing all the things that didn't require acknowledging my existence. I watched the stiffness of her shoulders, the way her hands moved a little too precisely, like she was concentrating very hard on not looking at me.

Maple took another microscopic bite of her cookie. "Do you make cookies every day?"

"Most days." Isla's voice was softer when she talked to Maple. Gentler. "Except Mondays. The bakery's closed on Mondays."

"What do you do on Mondays?"

"Sleep. Experiment with new recipes. Pretend I'm going to organize my apartment and then take a nap instead."

"Daddy's bad at organizing too. Our entire house is full of boxes. I wanna make a fort with them."

Isla's shoulders tensed. "Boxes?"

"Yeah. All our things are in them, which is why I can't make a fort yet, but—"

"Did you move back?" She directed the question to me, and I ran a hand through my hair and nodded.

"I'm surprised Dolores didn't tell you. That woman knows everything."

"How long ago?"

"Two months ago!" Maple's legs swung faster as she spoke. "We were staying at the farm with Uncle Levi, and there were chickens and goats and horses and cows and dogs and barn cats. The barn cats can't come inside. That's what Uncle Levi said. But we aren't living there anymore. We have a small house now. The boxes fill up the living room and I had, I had a dream that they tipped over and there was a big pile of stuff. Daddy's stuff and my stuff. And I went swimming in it. I'm starting kindergarten today, but then I ran away to come here because this bakery is the prettiest thing I've ever seen, and Daddy kept saying we'd come later, but later never comes, so I decided to make it now."

"Maple, eat your cookie," I murmured, nodding towards the cookie she'd nibbled like a mouse. When I glanced at Isla, she was standing with her hands on her hips, glaring at me. I rubbed the back of my neck. "Like she said, we've been back two months. Stayed with my brother until I got a lease. And we were supposed to be going to school, but Maple escaped from school drop-off. I'm still not sure how she did it. I looked away for half a second—"

"I'm sneaky," Maple announced proudly.

"You're grounded."

"What's grounded?"

"It's when you can't have dessert for a week."

Her face fell. "Oh. That's terrible. Can I be ungrounded if I finish all my vegetables?"

"We'll negotiate."

Isla had turned and stood with her back to us, hands braced on the counter, and tension ran up her spine. When she finally looked at me again, her expression was carefully neutral again, but her eyes were bright in a way that made my stomach clench.

"Well, I'm sure you've been busy." She nodded at Maple's cookie. "Enjoy sweetheart. And like I said, welcome back to town, Sawyer. I'm sure we'll run into each other again, since it's a small town and all. I'll do my best to make it less painful for both of us."

The dismissal was clear. I should leave. Take Maple, get back to the truck, drive away and go back to my carefully planned avoidance. But Maple was only halfway through her cookie, and she was finally, finally back to her happy self after two months of upheaval and custody threats and sleeping in unfamiliar places.

So I sat there while she ate, making appropriate noises at appropriate times while she chattered about cookie flavors and whether ghosts liked pumpkin spice. I tried not to watch Isla moving around her kitchen. Tried not to notice the way she still hummed under her breath when she worked. Tried not to think about the last time I'd seen her.

Tried and failed at all of it.

Maple finally finished, licking icing off her fingers. "Can we come back tomorrow?"

"We'll see."

"That means no." She sighed. "Grown-ups always say 'we'll see' when they mean no, but they think kids don't know that. We know that."

Before I could respond, my phone buzzed in my pocket. I pulled it out, glanced at the screen, and felt my stomach drop straight through the floor.

Unknown number. It was always bad news from unknown numbers these days.

The text was short.

> Mediation scheduled for October 21st, 9 AM. Bring proof of stable income and suitable childcare arrangements. Failure to appear will result in emergency custody evaluation.

I read it twice, trying to make the words say something different. They didn't.

Three weeks. I had three weeks to prove I deserved to keep my daughter. Three weeks to find a job that didn't involve mucking out stalls. Three weeks to establish childcare with people I barely knew anymore. Three weeks to convince a mediator that I was capable of being a single parent when I could barely manage to braid my daughter's hair without YouTube tutorials.

I looked up and found Isla watching me. Our eyes met and held for the first time since I'd walked through her door, and I watched her expression shift as she read whatever was on my face. The hardness softened, just barely, replaced by something that might have been concern if she weren't so determined to hate me.

"You okay?" The question came out reluctantly, like she'd tried to hold it back and failed.

"Yeah. Fine. Look, jellybean, we need to go. Come on."

Maple slid off her chair and made an elaborate curtsy toward Isla.

"Thank you for the magic cookie, Princess Isla. You're my new favorite person."

Isla curtsied back. "You're welcome, Princess Maple. You're my new favorite customer."

"Even better than the old ones?"

"Way better."

Maple beamed. She grabbed my hand and tugged me toward the door, chattering about how kindergarten was definitely going to be great now that she'd had a magic cookie for breakfast. I followed, letting her pull me along, and tried not to look back at Isla standing behind her counter with flour on her apron and questions in her eyes.

I failed at that too.

Outside, the October air was cool enough to make me wish I'd grabbed a jacket. The smell of wood smoke drifted from somewhere down the street, mixing with the scent of fallen leaves and distant rain. Main Street looked like a postcard of small-town autumn; pumpkins on stoops, scarecrows on benches, bunting in orange and black strung between lampposts. Picture perfect if you ignored the fact that my entire life was falling apart.

"Can we really come back?" Maple asked as I helped her into her booster seat.

"Maybe."

"That means no again, doesn't it?"

I buckled her in and pressed a kiss to the top of her head. Her hair smelled like the strawberry shampoo we'd used this morning, back when the worst thing I had to worry about was getting the braid straight. "That means I don't know yet. Let's get you to school before they send out a search party."

I closed her door, walked around to the driver's side, and let myself look back at the bakery one more time. Through the window, I could see Isla standing exactly where we'd left her, watching us. When she saw me looking, she turned away.

The story of us, really. One of us always turning away when the other one looked.

I started the truck—first try this time, small mercies—and pulled back onto Main Street. In the rearview mirror, Maple was already humming to herself, swinging her legs, completely unaware that she'd just torpedoed every plan I'd made since coming back to Acorn Field Heights.

My phone sat in the cup holder, the mediation text still glowing on the screen. October 21st.

The bakery disappeared behind us as I turned onto Oak Street. In three hours, I'd be back here to pick Maple up from her first day of kindergarten. In three weeks, I'd be sitting in the town hall with a mediator, fighting for the right to keep being her father.

Maybe I should've eaten a cookie too.

Read the rest of Sawyer and Isla's
story in the next book...

Cinnamon Kisses
& Forever Wishes

Make Sure To Check Out All 3 Cute Fall Romcoms With The Thatcher Brothers!

Make Sure To Check Out Maggie Ellis's First Christmas Novella

Acknowledgments

To my husband, who brings me blanks and delivers my favorite NON-pumpkin lattes. You are my favorite person and I love you.

Thank you to my sweet beta readers who made this book so much better with their incredible feedback, kind comments, and overall support: Rachel H., Becca L., and Jenn C.—you're the best kind of readers and even better friends.

And to my dog, who kept my feet warm as I planned out the Thatcher boy's books. Waiting patiently through every outline, every edit, and every coffee-fueled writing sprint isn't easy.

Of course, the biggest thank you is to you, wonderful reader. May your sweaters always be warm, your cider always spiced, and your autumn days always golden.

With love,

Maggie

IF YOU ENJOYED THIS SWEET FALL ROMCOM, PLEASE CONSIDER LEAVING A REVIEW. IT HELPS OUT A TON!

About the Author

Maggie Ellis writes swoony, clean romantic comedies filled with awkward meet-cutes, heartfelt moments, and more than a few cups of coffee. When she's not dreaming up cute romances, she can usually be found baking something unnecessarily complicated, wandering through independent bookstores, or losing another sock to the dryer gremlins. She lives in a small town where everyone waves and the Wi-Fi is questionable, but the inspiration is endless.

www.ingramcontent.com/pod-product-compliance
Lightning Source LLC
Chambersburg PA
CBHW021114130626
46554CB00002B/691